Foolproof LOVE

KATEE ROBERT

Entangled Publishing, LLC
2614 South Timberline Road
Suite 109
Fort Collins, CO 80525
Visit our website at www.entangledpublishing.com.

Brazen is an imprint of Entangled Publishing, LLC. For more information on our titles, visit www.brazenbooks.com.

Edited by Heather Howland
Cover design by Heather Howland
Cover art from DepositPhotos

Manufactured in the United States of America

First Edition June 2016

ENTANGLED
BRAZEN

To Kari. For our mutual love of growly country singers and dirty-talking cowboys.

Dear Reader,

It's been quite the journey to get this book into your hands. The Foolproof Love series was actually my first contracted category romance, way back in 2012, before *Wrong Bed, Right Guy* was ever a twinkle in my eye. It was originally supposed to be on the Indulgence line. Adam was a cold billionaire and Jules was a bartender. The book was good, but it just didn't work. In the intervening years, the story has worn many different suits, and none of them fit until I realized that my heroes simply must be cowboys.

Many things changed about this book, but Jules and Aubry's relationship never did. They are my single favorite lady relationship I've written to date. And Adam... Well, I hope you fall in love with him the same way I did. I fondly call this series my Dirty Talking Cowboys and he more than earns the title!

So settle in, clear your schedule, and let me introduce you to a little town in Texas called Devil's Falls. Our hero is a bull-rider and our heroine owns a cat café...

You're in for a treat!

Chapter One

"Tell me again why we're going out into the middle of nowhere for a bonfire? That's like holding up a sign *begging* some ax murder to come along and mass murder us."

Jules Rodriguez kept her eyes on the road—sad excuse that it was. Her truck rocked and shuddered as she muscled down the deep ruts. "We're not going to get mass murdered." Though her best friend, Aubry, had a point about it being in the middle of nowhere. They'd been working their way off the main road for almost twenty minutes, and there wasn't so much as a taillight in sight. She pushed down the knot of anxiety for the seventeen millionth time today.

"How do you know?"

Across the bench seat, her best friend had her knees pulled up to her chest and was staring out the side window like she expected that ax murder to come sprinting at the truck at any second. She wore her favorite pair of black jeans and one of her nerdy T-shirts with puns most people didn't understand, and she'd even picked out a pair of red tennis shoes instead of her normal boots.

Probably because she thinks she's going to have to run for her life at some point.

Aubry pointed at the passing trees. "I think I hear banjos."

"You live in Devil's Falls. I would think you'd be used to the banjos by now."

Aubry frowned, her pale face standing out against the darkness of the cab. Despite living in Texas for years, she managed to avoid anything that might resemble a tan. "I do my best to pretend they don't exist."

"Denial. It's not just a river in Egypt." She finally caught sight of light through the sparse trees. "There!"

Aubry pushed back her long, fire engine–red hair and snorted. "Who invited you to this thing again? Because if we're not going to be mass murdered—and I'm still not convinced on that note—they could be luring us in for some sacrificial killing."

"Has anyone ever told you that you have a deeply troubled obsession with murder?" Jules pulled in next to the open space at the end of a line of trucks. She recognized most of them from around town—Devil's Falls wasn't exactly a place hopping with new people. The last person to move in from out of town had been Aubry, and that was five years ago. "Besides, a sacrificial murder requires a virgin, and that ship sailed for both of us years ago."

"Good point." Aubry let loose a melodramatic sigh as she turned off the engine. "Remind me why we're doing this again?"

"Because Grant's back in town." Jules hadn't seen him since he dumped her ass on his way out of Devil's Falls after graduation—he hadn't even come back for holidays. Nine years later and his parting words were still ringing in her ears. *I don't want a life that's going to bore me into putting a gun in my mouth and pulling the trigger before I hit thirty.*

She clenched her hands around the steering wheel,

counting to ten twice. It didn't do a damn thing to stop the anger eating away at her. There wasn't a single thing wrong with Devil's Falls and the life she had here. Wanting to settle down and raise a family here—eventually—while being surrounded by the people she loved was a *good thing*. It didn't make her boring.

A subject she and Grant disagreed wholeheartedly on.

"Yeah, you mentioned that jackass showing up earlier, right before you started pummeling that poor loaf of bread at the café. Personally, I'm still waiting to hear what your plan is."

She didn't have one, not that she was going to let that stop her. It never had before. "I just want a look." Maybe he'd gained the freshman fifteen—and another twenty for law school. Or something. *Something* to prove that she was better off having been dumped so unceremoniously.

"I thought we agreed that your ex is a douchecanoe."

"We did. And I'm past it." Mostly. Past *him*, definitely. Past how he'd made her feel about herself, not so much.

Aubry snorted and opened the door. "Right. You're so past it that you've dragged us out to be maybe killed, maybe sacrificed to hang out with people who are still clinging desperately to their high school glory days." She looked around, her brows drawn together. "Because, seriously, who goes to bonfires when there's a perfectly adequate bar in town? *Two*, in fact."

"The cool kids?" That was always who'd been out at bonfires when she was in school. She'd avoided the whole scene, though, despite Grant's protests. They came out here as an excuse to drink without the town sheriff bothering them, and that had never been Jules's thing. She barely drank the hard stuff now, let alone when she was sixteen. And trying to navigate the roads back to town while buzzed? No, thanks.

That may or may not have also contributed to the whole

Jules-is-boring thing.

Aubry scrunched her nose. "Ten to one, someone's wearing a decade-old letterman's jacket and talking about that one football game where he threw the winning pass."

Ten to one it's Grant himself.

Jules looped her arm through her best friend's. "An hour. After that, we can go back to town, grab a bottle of wine, and play that horribly violent game that you love so much."

"Deal." Aubry grinned. "And don't act so put-upon. You love it as much as I do—you just suck at it."

"Truth." She pulled them to a stop at the edge of the clearing. There were trucks parked in here around the fire, too, their tailgates down and people situated around them, chatting and drinking and a few women even dancing. It looked like something straight out of a country music video. She picked out a dozen people she'd gone to high school with, the ones who'd stayed behind and never wanted to leave, and another dozen who had left with stars in their eyes but had filtered back into town in the years since graduation.

"Jules? Jules Rodriguez?"

She froze. There was no mistaking Grant's deep voice. *Too soon. I'm not ready.* But since the only other option was dropping Aubry's arm and fleeing into the night, she turned around with a smile pasted on her face. And there he was, standing a few feet away, his dark hair shorter than she remembered. No freshman fifteen there. Damn it. He looked like he'd been spending quite a bit of time in the gym, in fact.

Bet he spends the whole time he's working out checking himself out in the mirror.

The snarky thought didn't make her feel any better. There was nothing worse than being caught flat-footed by the ex who left her in the dust, only to find out that he hadn't developed some unfortunate skin problem in the intervening years.

"Grant."

He moved closer. "Damn, you're a sight for sore eyes. You look good, Jules."

"Oh, you know, Pilates," she answered breezily, already searching the crowd around them for an escape. She cleared her throat. "So, uh, how are things?"

"Great. Better than great. I just graduated from Duke. Top of my class." He gave a smile that was all teeth, like a politician. "I have a position waiting for me in my father's firm here in town."

"Imagine that." She couldn't even bring herself to pretend to be surprised. Grant always had been fond of riding his daddy's coattails. For all that he was determined to live the big life off in Anywhere but Devil's Falls, he liked being a big fish in a little pond more.

"And you? I think I heard that you opened up some sort of cat café?" He laughed. "Can't say that's surprising."

Beside her, Aubry went ramrod straight. It was only a matter of time before her friend went postal on his ass. Jules smiled, and though she wanted to holler at him something fierce, she managed to keep her tone even. She was *not* ashamed of Cups and Kittens. "It's been a real hit with the locals."

"I bet." He looked her over, head to toe and back again. His appraising gaze made her skin crawl. "I hear you're still single. You want to go get a drink sometime?"

Suddenly, Jules was a whole lot less worried about keeping Aubry back than she was about pressing her lips together to keep from laying into him. She looked around at the people circling the bonfire. A full half of them were watching this little drama play out.

Did he seriously just ask me out?

No. No, absolutely not. Nope. Never.

She had to do something, and fast. Jules wasn't a particularly violent person, but she also wasn't above hunting down Grant's truck and slitting the tires.

And maybe scrawling something witty in the paint with her keys.

No. That's not going to solve anything, and you'll just prove to him and everyone else that he can still get under your skin without even trying.

There had to be a better way to put him in his place.

Her gaze landed on her cousin across the way. Daniel stood next to a lowered tailgate next to his friend Quinn. And with them was a tall drink of water if she ever saw one. He had his back to her, but the way his shoulders filled out his T-shirt, tapering down to a lean waist and... Good lord, his pants were the very definition of painted-on jeans. Daniel said something, and he shook his head, turning so she could see his granite jawline and...

She blinked.

Holy shit, it's Adam Meyers.

He'd been around while she was growing up, always running with her cousin and their other two friends, but he'd always seemed wilder than the other boys—more restless. Even when he was standing still, there was a look in his eye like he was just waiting for the right moment to burst into motion.

Sure enough, the first chance he got, he blew out of town and up and joined the rodeo. Or that was the word on the Devil's Falls gossip grapevine.

He must be back in town to take care of his mom. Sympathy rose, blotting out her anger at Grant. Jules didn't know what was wrong with his mom, but she didn't have to be a doctor to know the woman was sick.

Knowing him, though, he won't stick around for long.

Just like that, a plan clicked into place. A stupid, reckless plan guaranteed to shut Grant down for at least a little while.

Speaking of, he was still waiting for her to say yes and

fulfill his high-handed expectations, but she managed a laugh. "That's really sweet, Grant. It was great seeing you, but my *boyfriend* is waiting for me."

He frowned. "Boyfriend?"

"Oh, yeah, it's a new thing. We haven't exactly gone public with it—you know how Devil's Falls can be—so you wouldn't have heard." She gave him a pat on his arm. "It was nice seeing you. So great. Really, we'll have to catch up sometime soon." And then she stepped around him, dragging Aubry behind her.

"What are you doing?" Aubry whispered.

"Winging it." She stopped by the trio of men, all too aware of Grant watching her. "Hi, Daniel. Quinn. Adam."

They raised their beers. Daniel looked over her shoulder with a frown. "Is that your piece-of-shit ex-boyfriend I see?"

"The very one." She disentangled her arm from Aubry's. "Speaking of, I need a favor."

"Anything for you, kid."

She tried not to roll her eyes at him calling her kid. He was a whole seven years older than her. Not exactly ancient. "Actually, it's not you I need the favor from."

Before she could talk herself out of it, she sidled up to Adam and put her arms around his neck. To his credit, he didn't shove her on her butt in the dirt, merely raising his eyebrows. Jules kept her voice low so there was no chance of Grant overhearing. "So as you've noticed, my ex is watching me really closely right now, and I might have told him a tiny white lie about me dating someone in order to avoid a devastating dose of humiliation. And since I can't date Daniel and no one would *ever* believe I'd date Quinn—"

The man in question frowned. "You really know how to hit a man where it hurts, Jules."

"—that leaves you."

Adam's face remained impassive. "I see."

There wasn't a whole lot to work with in those words, but he also had let his free hand drift down to settle on her hip, so she just kept talking. "If you could just play along and maybe kiss me like you want to do filthy things to me in the bed of your truck, I'd really appreciate it."

If anything, his eyebrows rose higher. "That guy really got under your skin, didn't he?"

"You have no idea."

Next to them, Daniel made a sound suspiciously like a growl, but neither of them looked over. Adam's hand pulsed on her hip, the heat of it shocking despite the warmth of the night. His calluses dragged over the sensitive skin bared by her T-shirt, and she shivered. *Maybe this was a terrible idea.*

She didn't have time to really reconsider, though, because he set down his beer, cupped the back of her neck, and dealt her the single most devastating kiss of her life. No, not a kiss. He took *possession* of her mouth, his tongue tracing the seam of her lips and then delving inside. He tasted of beer and something darker, something that hinted at exactly what she'd asked for—like he wanted to do filthy things to her in the bed of his truck.

She closed her eyes, giving his tongue a tentative stroke, and had to fight down a moan at the way the move made her entire body go tight.

More.

He lifted his head, breaking the kiss and slamming her back into the real world. She blinked up at him, all too aware of her body pressed against the entirety of his, of how he was hard in all the places she was soft, of how goddamn *good* he smelled. "Wow."

There went that eyebrow again. "You think it was believable?"

She'd almost forgotten she was kissing Adam Meyers because he was supposed to be her boyfriend to prove a point to her real ex-boyfriend. *Liar. You 100 percent forgot that this was pretend, and if he'd offered to drive you out into a field to get down and dirty, you wouldn't even hesitate.*

He *hadn't* offered, and this *was* pretend. Remembering that was important if she wanted to avoid compounding one potentially humiliating situation with another even more potentially humiliating situation.

She licked her lips. "Um, yes. Totally believable. Thank you."

He still didn't let her go. Instead he turned and lifted her onto the tailgate as if she weighed no more than a paper doll. "You want something to drink?"

"Uh, sure." She should get down and walk away...which she absolutely would do as soon as she got control of her shaking legs. It would have taken a stronger woman than she was to not stare at Adam's ass in those tight jeans as he ambled over to the cooler.

She turned to find Aubry doing a silent slow clap. "Don't judge me."

"Oh, I'm judging."

Chapter Two

Adam Meyers had been back in Devil's Falls all of two days, and he was already going out of his mind.

He hadn't wanted to come to this goddamn bonfire. He wasn't back in Devil's Falls for a good time—he wasn't even back at all. Once he figured out what was going on with his mama, he was on the road again. Hell, it had only been a few days, and the restlessness in his blood was already snapping for a change of scenery.

Or it had been until Jules Rodriguez sidled up to him and proceeded to rock his world. That'd been a distraction he couldn't afford to pass up.

He opened the cooler and fished out a pair of beers, using the move to get his physical reaction under control. He hadn't expected to be affected like that, but she was so soft and sweet and the panic in her dark eyes had called to him.

You were doing her a favor, jackass.

Right. He glanced over his shoulder to where she was talking to the redhead. *I'd like to do her another favor. Maybe two.*

"Damn it, what are you doing?"

He'd known this was coming the second he walked away from the women. He couldn't even blame Daniel. His friend had always had been overprotective of Jules.

Adam used his boot to shut the cooler lid. "She asked me for a favor. I'd be a dick to ignore her cry for help."

"That's my baby cousin."

Cousin or not, the soft, sexy woman he'd just held in his arms was *not* a baby. Not even close. He snorted. "It's not like I'm robbing the cradle here. And it was just a kiss."

"You know damn well it was a bad idea." When Adam just stared, Daniel cursed. "Damn it, Adam. It better *stop* at just a kiss." He stalked away, snagging a beer as he did.

He didn't blame his friend for getting up in arms. Jules had always been a good girl, and Adam was many things, but good wasn't on the list. Which was most likely why she'd chosen him to act as her pretend boyfriend.

Adam turned around to find Grant standing just out of reach. He hadn't had much interaction with the guy—by the time Grant graduated seven years behind him, Adam had already blown out of town for the rodeo circuit. His mama told him stories, though. It was one of her favorite things to do on their weekly calls while he was traveling around and getting into trouble. The tidbits of Devil's Falls gossip had always grounded him. No matter how crazy his life got, or how free he felt on the back of a bull for those precious seconds before he was thrown, nothing much changed back home.

That was how he knew Grant and Jules had dated through high school and that he'd dumped her before he went off to that fancy school his daddy had paid out the nose for. It wasn't something Adam had put much thought into all those years ago, but now he had to stop and wonder what the hell Jules had seen in this guy.

Grant was too polished, too put together. Even his teeth

were perfect, white and straight and screaming money. It made sense. His daddy was a big fish in Devil's Falls, and he'd never let anyone forget it. Stood to reason that his son inherited his shitty, entitled attitude.

And he was obviously chewing on something he wanted to say.

Adam stopped, aware of Quinn at his back. He doubted this preppy man was going to cause problems, but if he got a wild hair, he'd find that it was two on one. "Can I help you?"

"You're Adam Meyers."

"Guilty."

Grant shot a look over his shoulder to where Jules sat on Adam's tailgate, her long legs swinging as she chatted with her redhead friend. There was nothing over the top sexy about the way she was dressed—shorts and a plaid long-sleeved shirt that she'd rolled up to her elbows—but she drew Adam's gaze despite that. There was just something so *alive* about her.

He needed to feel alive right about now.

Adam started moving forward again, tired of the game and surprisingly eager to get back to Jules. Maybe he should kiss her again. *You know, for believability's sake.* "Excuse me."

"Wait." Grant grabbed his shoulder and smiled. There was nothing overtly wrong with the expression, but the fact he was touching him—holding him back—left Adam wanting to punch some of those too-perfect teeth out.

"I suggest removing your hand before I remove it for you."

Grant's smile didn't waver, but he *did* drop his hand. "I know the score."

What the fuck was he talking about? "Good for you."

"I mean, it's cute that you're helping Jules make me jealous, but it's not going to work."

He knew that kiss had been a desperate Hail Mary pass at saving face, but that didn't mean he was going to sell her out. It didn't hurt Adam none to play along—and, yeah, he wouldn't mind another chance to taste Jules again. She was dynamite, and he'd never been able to resist playing with matches. "Don't know what you're talking about."

"Oh, please." Grant rolled his eyes. "A few years might have passed, but that doesn't change the fact that I *know* Jules. There's no way in hell she's dating you."

"How do you figure?"

He knew where this was going. Despite his mama's best efforts, he'd been hell on wheels while he was growing up. He had too much anger, too much energy, and a chip on his shoulder a mile wide. All that combined into giving him a reputation that kept his mama up at night.

So he'd left, needing to see more of the world than this hole-in-the-wall little town. The world was too big, too full of life, to stay in one place too long. He'd hit the jackpot when he decided to try the rodeo, and that first time riding a bull had ignited something in him he couldn't resist. The second he'd picked himself up after being thrown, he'd craved another ride.

That craving hadn't disappeared over the years.

If anything, it'd only gotten stronger.

He'd put all that aside the second Lenora called him to tell him his mama was in a bad way. It hadn't been comfortable driving back into Devil's Falls—like sliding into a suit that was two sizes too small—but it didn't matter. His mama needed him, so here he was.

Grant shifted, as if just now realizing he could be getting himself into the kind of trouble that wasn't easy to get out of. "Nothing against you, of course. It's just that she's…Jules. She takes the safe road. She's a sweet girl, but she's, well, you know." He waved a hand in her direction. "A bit boring."

Adam focused on controlling the rushing in his ears. Fifteen years ago, he would have punched Grant's lights out just for saying something so goddamn stupid. He was different now.

More or less.

He moved forward, getting into the man's space. "That's my girlfriend you're talking about."

Grant went pale, his mouth opening and closing like a fish's out of water. "You're joking."

"Get out of my sight, *boy*."

Under different circumstances, it would have been funny to see how fast Grant hightailed it around the bonfire, but Adam was too busy trying to get a handle on the anger whipping through him. It was like a live thing in his chest, demanding physical action. He took a deep breath, and then another, wrestling it back under control. "I hate that guy."

"Man, chill." Quinn took one of the beers out of Adam's hand and popped the top, then repeated the process with the other. "Remember what the sheriff said about fighting—you promised to behave."

"That was when we were teenagers."

"Same rule applies. Sheriff Taylor is getting old and has high blood pressure. You don't want to be going and giving him a heart attack, now do you?"

Adam shot Quinn a look, but he took the beer back. "You're an idiot."

"Nah, I'm the smart one." He gave a lazy grin. "Though if we stand here any longer while there are two gorgeous girls waiting for us, then someone might have a legit argument about the idiot thing."

He glanced at the girls…and his cock jumped to attention. Jules was now leaning against the tailgate. The frayed edges of her shorts teased a peek of the lower curve of her ass. He was sure they'd started as something closer to modest, but they'd been washed so many times, they taunted him as she walked away, as if they'd fray just a bit more and give him the show of his life. "Those shorts should be illegal," he muttered.

"What's that?" Quinn asked.

"Nothing." Just past the girls, Adam spotted Daniel heading toward the line of trucks disappearing into the darkness. Back when they were kids, Daniel had been the straitlaced one. The one who got them out of as much trouble as Adam and John got them into. *John.* It had all changed that night on the rain-slicked road. "How's he doing? Really doing?"

"Hell, man, I don't know. It all changed when you left." There was no accusation in Quinn's voice, but Adam felt it all the same.

After John died, he should have stayed to help pick up the pieces. He knew Daniel blamed himself for the car crash, but he'd been so desperate to get out of town, he'd barely paused long enough to fill up his truck before he headed for the horizon. He hadn't even made the funeral. And he hadn't come back much in the intervening years—definitely not long enough to get past the nights of drunken partying with his buddies.

I'm back now, at least for a couple weeks, and I'm going to set shit right.

That started with the woman now watching him across the clearing with dark eyes. He had no business sniffing around Jules Rodriguez, if only because she was Daniel's cousin, and he'd failed his friend enough without adding this to the list. But Adam couldn't get the image of her desperate expression out of his head.

He couldn't hang her out to dry. Not tonight, at least.

He walked over and passed over a beer before he joined her against the tailgate. There was a respectable distance between them, but he still was acutely aware of every move she made. When she lifted the beer to sip it, Adam damn near groaned.

Jules's gaze fell to the bottle in her hands. "He didn't believe the kiss, did he?"

Adam took a long pull on his beer bottle, more to calm himself down than because he was thirsty. "He had his doubts."

"Damn." She sighed, her shoulders slumping. "Thanks for trying. A-plus for effort."

There wasn't going to be a clearer opening. That kiss had been the sole moment since he'd been back in town where he wasn't ready to climb the walls. She was *right there*, the perfect distraction all wrapped up in a package that seemed designed to make him sit up and take notice.

It would be a shitty thing to do. No.

But when he opened his mouth, different words came out. "I guess we'll just have to be more convincing."

The redhead on the other side of Jules made a choking sound. "Oh my God, you're crazier than she is."

Jules's mouth opened into a little O, and her eyes went wide. "I'm sorry, what?"

This was his chance to take it all back—all he had to do was let her down easy—but apparently Adam was too much of a selfish bastard for that. He leaned in, almost close enough to touch. "You up to giving him a little show? I can do this all night."

She bit her lip, her gaze dropping to his mouth. "That's really sweet, but I can't ask you to do that. I've already sexually assaulted you once tonight. I doubt my conscience can handle more."

"It's no trouble." Why was he pushing this? He couldn't force Jules into it, though, so he just toasted her with his beer. "Think about it."

"Oh, she's going to think about it, all right." The redhead dodged the elbow aimed her way this time. "I'm just going to, ah, mosey on over there and find myself a drink that's more of the vodka variety."

Quinn appeared at her shoulder like some kind of magician. "I got it." He presented her a red Solo cup with a flourish. "Tell me, sweet cheeks, did it hurt when you fell from heaven?"

"Nope, but I scraped my knees when I crawled up from hell." The woman rattled off her response without looking at him or sounding the least bit interested.

Quinn, on the other hand, only seemed more intrigued. "Witty. I like that. Maybe you and me should go get a drink sometime."

Jules coughed, and Adam had to use every ounce of willpower under his control to keep his grin off his face when the redhead turned to his friend, made a show of looking him up and down, and shook her head. "Sorry, cowboy, but judging from the assets you're far too proud of displaying"—she waved at his crotch area—"I've had better. Not interested."

She turned to Jules. "Can we please leave? Much more of this and I'm going to develop a sudden infatuation with my cousin."

"God forbid." Jules shifted away from the tailgate and shot a smile at Adam. "Thanks for the beer and, well, for everything else, too. You're sweet." Then she was gone, being towed by her friend through the crowd back toward the line of trucks.

Adam sipped his beer, watching her pivot her hips to avoid a drunk guy. The move made his cock perk up—again—and take notice. As if he hadn't been interested before.

He didn't look over when his friend took her place, even when Quinn said, "I love me some redheads—so snarky and full of rage."

"You're a sick, sick man."

"No doubt." He drained his beer and set it aside. "So what's your next step?"

He glanced over. "What do you mean?"

"Come on, man. I know you, and I've seen that look on your face before—usually when you're about to get me into a whole world of trouble. You're not done with that woman."

"She said she wasn't interested." His gaze tracked back to the trucks, craving another look at the way she filled out those damn shorts.

"Right." Quinn snorted. "Whatever you say."

Chapter Three

Jules stepped over Mr. Winkles and made her way to the table where Mrs. Peterson was petting Cujo while she read the morning paper. "I hear that boyfriend of yours is back in town, dear."

"Ex-boyfriend." She dodged Cujo's clawed swipe and topped off the old woman's coffee.

"I also hear that his daddy is planning on grooming him to take over the family business. Very prestigious, that." She still didn't look up from her paper.

Jules gritted her teeth and made an effort to keep the smile on her face. "I really wouldn't know." *You know she's just poking for gossip. There's no malice behind it.*

It didn't make it sting any less, though.

She'd known everyone would start with the questions the second Grant got back into town. It might have been nearly a decade, but the Devil's Falls residents weren't much a fan of change. They'd liked it when Jules and Grant were Jules-and-Grant, the town's golden couple, and most would be tickled pink if the two of them picked up where they left off.

Obviously kissing Adam hasn't hit the grapevine yet.

Jules cleared her throat at the thought. "Would you like a blueberry muffin?" she asked. "They just came out of the oven."

"Oh, I really shouldn't."

They went through this same song and dance every day. Jules smiled. There was comfort in knowing what to expect, no matter what Grant believed. "If you're sure. There's banana nut, too."

Mrs. Peterson froze like a hound catching a scent. "Banana nut, you say? Well, maybe just this once."

"Be right back." She turned around, pausing to pet Loki and Rick where they were sunning themselves in a beam of light coming through the big windows in the front of the shop. They rewarded her with rumbling purrs, and Loki even managed to rouse himself to bump his head against her leg. She scratched behind his ears the way he liked.

The locals had given her grief when she bought this place and announced it was going to be a cat café, though it was the kind of indulgent grief she was used to. *Oh, that Jules Rodriguez—she's so* quirky. But when it came to the café, the proof was in the pudding, and over the course of any given week, most of them made some excuse or other to walk through the doors and cuddle one of the seven cats she kept here. It might be a little strange to some people, but this coffee shop made people happy, and that made *Jules* happy.

What was so wrong with that?

She delivered the banana nut to Mrs. Peterson and then started a new pot of coffee, her mind going back to the events of the night before as she went through the familiar motions.

Kissing Adam Meyer had been... Well, it had been a questionable plan at best. She'd wanted to create a scandal, and once news of that kiss hit town, scandal was exactly what she'd get.

She dumped the water into the machine, her body prickling with awareness she had no idea what to do with. The kiss had been pretend. She knew that rationally, but her hormones were having problems remembering it.

Especially when he'd offered to keep the charade going. *I can do this all night.*

The awareness grew stronger, sparking in places it had no business being. The man was just doing her a favor, and all she could think about was how good he smelled and how sexy it had been to feel his whiskers scraping against her skin? Her imagination was all too willing to offer up ideas about where else they would feel good if she'd given him all night.

Stop it.

She slammed the pot into its place with more force than necessary. There was no reason Adam would be interested in her as anything other than a charity case, which was reason enough to thank him again for taking one for the team and then move on with her life. She didn't want charity from anyone.

She needed to stop trying to prove to Grant that she wasn't pathetic. She shouldn't even *care* what he thought—what anyone thought. She wasn't a pushover. Her life was great…minus her failed attempts in the romance department. Otherwise, she saw what she wanted, and she worked hard to get it. She'd be totally content working Cups and Kittens until she was old and gray, living in the apartment above it with Aubry, and sitting out on the balcony and waving her cane at the teenagers in the street…

"Oh my God, I'm pathetic."

"Talking to yourself is a sure sign of insanity." Aubry spoke from the corner table where she was doing something on her massive laptop—probably plotting world domination. Or gaming.

She pushed the button to start the coffee brewing,

breathing in the comforting smell and doing her best to get her crazy under control. "Wrong. There are studies showing that talking to yourself is a sign of intelligence." *Thank you, Facebook.*

"Touché." Aubry glanced up and her eyes went wide. "Incoming."

Jules turned around in time to see Grant open the door to the shop. Her stomach took a nosedive. She spun back around, pretending she hadn't seen him, and busied herself with the coffeepot to buy time. She'd bet her last dollar that he was here to call her out on faking Adam being her boyfriend. Grant had never been able to let stuff like that go.

What had she seen in that guy again?

Oh, right. Popular high school football player who had turned that golden charm on her sixteen-year-old self and made her feel like something really special.

Until he crushed her under his shoe as he left her in the dust.

"Hey, Jules."

She couldn't keep pretending she didn't see him when he was trying to engage her in conversation. Jules turned. "Grant. What a surprise."

He smirked. "There's a bell over the door."

"I was talking about you showing up in the first place." She shot a look at where Mrs. Peterson had Cujo in her lap and wasn't even pretending not to eavesdrop. Jules gritted her teeth. "Can I help you with something?"

"So this is your place." He made a show of looking around. "It's…quaint."

She followed his gaze, trying to see things through his point of view. The shop was decent sized, with plenty of room for half a dozen tables and the long counter that she stood behind, as well as three elaborate cat towers. The walls were a cheery blue, and there were suns painted onto the tabletops.

It was a bright and happy place and damn him to hell for trying to make her embarrassed of it.

Power through it. You can do this. "Would you like some coffee?"

"Oh, no, thanks. I'm heading to the Starbucks down the street." He smiled his million-dollar smile. "I just came by to check the place out. And because I'd hoped you reconsidered that date."

Fury temporarily stole her words. First the Starbucks comment, and now this again? He didn't get to just waltz back into town and pick her up like she was a forgotten toy. She clenched her hands, forcibly reminding herself that assaulting customers wasn't a good way to bring in business. Plus, she was *nice*. Nice girls didn't smash coffeepots over the heads of their ex-boyfriends.

But even nice girls stood their ground. She lifted her chin. "As I think I made more than clear last night, I'm seeing someone."

"Somehow, I'm not so sure about that." He tipped an imaginary hat and walked out the door, still grinning.

She should have known pretending to date Adam would backfire. Now, not only was she *quirky* for staying in a small town and owning a cat café, but she was pathetic for pretending to date someone and it being clear to Grant and everyone else that there was no way Adam Meyers would really date her. Why would he? He was exciting and wild and hot. And she was Jules Rodriguez, local good girl and budding cat lady.

"I hate that Grant makes me feel like this. Still."

Aubry opened her mouth, but whatever she was going to say was lost when she laughed. "Incoming two point oh."

"Did I do something to anger the fates? Because this is freaking ridiculous."

She braced herself for another go-round with Grant, but

it wasn't his outline darkening her doorstep.

No, it was Adam's.

Her heart leaped into her throat, even as she told herself it was a completely unforgivable reaction. He'd done her a favor last night. End of story.

But that didn't stop her body from perking up and taking notice of every move he made. It wasn't how he walked in and instantly took control of the room without even doing anything. He filled the doorway, and though he wasn't as tall as Quinn, there was nothing small or short about Adam. *I wonder...*

Nope. Knock that right off.

She was nearly 100 percent sure he wasn't wearing the same jeans from last night, because these hugged his thighs, showcasing the muscles that flexed with each step, leading up to... *Oh, my.* She sent a silent little thank-you to whoever designed the jeans, because they were so fitted, it was pretty darn clear that he was perfectly in proportion *everywhere*.

She jerked her gaze to his face, but that didn't help at all, because all she could see was the square jaw, his dark eyes, and his mouth. The very same mouth she'd been kissing less than twenty-four hours ago.

Jules licked her lips. If she concentrated, she could almost taste him there.

She watched Adam carefully pick his way across the coffee shop, doing his best not to trip over Khan and Loki and Ninja Kitteh as they came to investigate the new customer. The three cats refused to take a hint, though. They rubbed on his legs, purring up a storm and making it generally impossible to take a step without trampling one of them. She bit her lip to keep from laughing at the exasperated look on his face.

He finally took a massive step over them and strode to the counter before they could catch up. "Hey, Jules."

"Hi." Did her voice sound breathy? She was pretty sure

it sounded breathy. She knew Adam more by reputation than anything else, but he didn't seem so bad the few times they'd encountered each other. "Can I get you something?"

"Coffee would be great. Black, please." He frowned when Khan leaped onto the counter and put his front paws on Adam's chest, demanding to be adored. "A cat café, huh?"

The embarrassment she'd almost cured herself of after Grant left came back double-time. She focused on pouring him a cup of coffee. "What is so wrong about owning my own business? It's something a lot of people aspire to, and the fact that mine just happens to be a little *quirky* doesn't make it less of an accomplishment." She turned around to find that damned eyebrow raised again. "What?"

"Well, hell, sugar, I wasn't criticizing." He looked around, still petting Khan. "It's a neat idea."

"Oh." She passed over the mug, feeling stupid. "Sorry. Everyone keeps hinting at Grant and me getting back together, and then Grant himself stopped by, and I guess I'm just riled up."

His mouth tightened. "That guy's an asshole. And everyone else is, too, if they expect you to fall all over him again. You deserve better, Jules."

She blinked. What was she supposed to say to that? "Er… thank you." *Lame.* She shook her head when he reached for his wallet. "It's on the house. For last night."

"Anytime." He leaned against the counter, which was too freaking close to hip height for her peace of mind, and lowered his voice. "And I do mean anytime."

There was no mistaking the invitation in his voice. Her stomach fluttered and her inner devil's advocate kicked into high gear.

It wasn't so bad pretending to be his girlfriend. You could do it again.

She told that little voice to shut up, but it wasn't listening.

Maybe this is exactly what you need to shake up the town's perception of you.

That got her attention.

What she really wanted—more than shutting down Grant—was a chance to prove that she hadn't been put on the shelf when he left her behind. She *wasn't* the early-spinster cat lady they all suspected, darn it. Maybe she could kill two birds with one stone by continuing this. Pretending to date Adam last night was all well and good, but it didn't hold up to the light of day—not unless they *made* it hold up. She drummed her fingers on the counter, watching him drink his coffee and eyeball the cat. If they kept it up for a week or two…it might work.

There's also the added benefit of more kissing.

"Adam…" She glanced over, and realized Mrs. Peterson was staring at them, once again not even trying to pretend she wasn't eavesdropping. *Crap.* "Aubry, can you watch the counter for a few?"

"Sure."

She gave Adam a bright smile. "Can I talk to you privately? You can bring Khan."

He scooped up the orange tom with one hand and his coffee with the other. "You named a cat after a *Star Trek* villain."

"Guilty." She opened the door to the back. "The others are Cujo, Loki, Rick, Dog, Ninja Kitteh, and Mr. Winkles."

He laughed. "That's a whole lot of pop culture wrapped up into tiny bundles."

"Hey, the names fit."

"I bet they do."

She stopped in the kitchen and made an effort not to wring her hands. *The worst he can say is no.* "So, uh, thanks again for doing me that favor last night."

He paced around the kitchen, seeming to take in

everything as he stroked Khan's back. "It was really no problem. Kissing beautiful women isn't exactly a hardship."

He thinks I'm... She rushed on, refusing to dwell on that. He had to say something nice. He was Daniel's friend, after all. "So, it goes like this—Grant is a giant asshole."

"Agreed." He made another circuit around the kitchen, pausing to poke at the cat-shaped cookie cutters she had out on the counter for the batch of sugar cookies she was baking later.

So far, so good. "When he dumped me and left town, he basically said the reason we couldn't be together was that he wanted to be with someone more exciting—someone who wanted more out of life than to live and die in a small town."

He turned to face her, his jaw tight. "Calling him an asshole might be too kind."

"He's hardly the only one who's ever said that to me, but that's beside the point. Everyone in this town thinks I'm destined to be a spinster. I'm not. At least, I hope I'm not. But I have no way to prove it, and I'm sick of them thinking my sole purpose in life should be to win Grant back. So, here's the thing." Time for the pitch. "If your offer still stands, I'd really, really like it if you'd keep pretending to be my boyfriend— and really give Devil's Falls something to talk about."

Adam blinked. "I'm sorry, what? I think I misheard you over the sound of this fellow's purring. I thought you just said that you want to use me to stir up the gossip mill in town."

That was the part he'd decide to focus on? "You did."

"How the hell am I supposed to do that?"

"I don't know. You're Adam Meyer—bull rider and Devil's Falls legend. You have excitement in your blood."

He stared at her, still for the first time since they walked back to the kitchen.

She sighed. "You're right. It's a dumb idea. I have a ton of them. It's a sickness."

"Wait, wait." He set the cat down and took a drink of his coffee. "You know if I'm going to be your boyfriend, we can't do it halfway."

Now *she* was sure she'd heard *him* wrong. "I'm sorry, what?"

"This is Devil's Falls. The only thing the people here love more than ranching is good gossip, which can work against you as easily as you want it to work for you. If even one person thinks we aren't serious, it'll be impossible to convince them you shouldn't crawl back to golden-boy Grant."

She was almost afraid to hope she was hearing him right. "You...you'll do it?" But then her brain caught up to everything he'd said. "Wait, what do you mean?"

His grin made her stomach leap. "We'll give them something to talk about. Something to show them you're 100 percent over that jackass."

That was what she wanted. It was just daunting when her mind was all too eager to offer up exactly *what* they could do to get the town talking and defuse the whole Jules-and-Grant fantasy. It would have to be pretty scandalous. She picked up Khan, holding him to her chest like a furry shield, though she couldn't say what she wanted protection from. "You're really agreeing to this?"

"Hell, sugar, I could never turn down a woman in need, and you fit the bill."

She could barely believe it. Crazy schemes were her and Aubry's thing, but maybe they were Adam's, too. "Thank you. Oh God, thank you so much. I owe you..." She looked around for inspiration. "Free coffee for life?"

He laughed. "I wouldn't say no to free coffee for the duration of my time here." He lifted his mug. "This is amazing."

"Thanks." She frowned. It seemed crass to ask him straight out how his mom was doing, especially since he hadn't offered up any information to begin with. "How long are you back for?"

"Not sure yet." A shadow passed over his face, but his expression was so closed down, she didn't dare risk pissing him off by pushing for more information. It must've been worse than Jules thought.

She almost backed out right then, because if Adam was dealing with his mom being *really* sick, wasn't playing along with her scheme the last thing he needed? She hesitated. *It's not up to me to decide what he needs. He's offering me something* I *need right now, and this is the best opportunity I'm going to get—the* only *opportunity.* Jules stuck out her hand. "Deal?"

Adam set his coffee cup down and took her hand. "Deal."

Chapter Four

"A date? You've been back in town for two whole days. How in God's name did you manage to sweet-talk some local girl into letting you take her out?"

Adam opened the pillbox and carefully took out the half a dozen pills in varying sizes and colors and set them on the counter. "You know me, Mama. I work fast."

His mom laughed, the chuckle a whole lot weaker than her usual boisterous sound. Everything about her was weaker now. The cancer that she'd hidden for far too long had eaten away at her body, leaving her a shell of the woman he'd grown up with.

Regret bit him, hard and fast. The only reason he knew that she had cancer at all was because her lady friend, Lenora, had called him. He was still pissed the fuck off that he had to hear about it from the woman she was dating rather than his mama herself. Pissed off, but not surprised. He should have been here, making sure she was taking care of herself. He knew damn well that his mama would work herself to the bone to make everyone else around her happy. Combined with her general distrust of doctors, it was a recipe for disaster. If he'd been here, he would have known that something was wrong and insisted she go in and get checked out.

"Oh, dear. I know that look." She patted his arm. "Stop it. There's nothing you could have done."

"Mama—"

"Tell me about this girl. Is she anyone I know?"

Just like that, the discussion was over before it began. They'd have to talk about it at some point, but he wasn't willing to fight with her—not while she looked like a stiff wind might topple her over. "Jules Rodriguez."

"Danny's little cousin?" Her eyes lit up. "She's got that wonderful coffee shop with all the cats. I go in there once a week with Lenora. That Loki is a darling." She accepted the tall glass of water he'd filled for her, some censure creeping into her dark eyes. "She's a nice girl, Adam."

"I know." He braced himself for what would come next.

Sure enough, his mama said, "If I thought for a second you were going to hold still long enough to put down roots, I'd keep my thoughts to myself, but you're as footloose and fancy-free as that father of yours."

Of all the things she could have said, this one stung the most. Because it was true. He set the pills in front of her. "I'm staying long enough to get you sorted out, Mama. I promise."

"Oh, honey…" Tears filled her eyes, tears that felt like they were ripping into his very soul. There was a terrible knowledge on her face that he wasn't ready to face. Not now—maybe not ever. His mom managed a smile. "I love you."

That was it. There was nothing else he could say. "I love you, too." He waited through the torturous process of her taking her pills, and then watched her with an eagle eye while she walked back into the living room and her recliner.

She shot him a sharp look. "I've been getting around just fine on my own before you got back, Adam Christopher. I don't need you hovering."

"In that case, I'll be going."

He hesitated by the door and looked at his mama. She used to be larger than life, a formidable woman who stood between him and the rest of the world. And here he was, leaving her again. It didn't matter that it was for a date instead of the rodeo, or that she was practically kicking him out the door. He should be here.

"Go, Adam."

As always, she knew what he was thinking without him saying it. He forced a smile. He could be positive if that's what she wanted, at least until he got some concrete answers. "Do you want me to bring anything back?"

"I'm fine. Go on your date." She waved him away.

He went, but he could feel her eyes on his back the entire time, and her words rang in his ears. The thought of settling down in one place was enough to have him breaking out in hives. It was a small part of the toxicity that had been Adam as a teenager—the desire to go anywhere but here, to get in a truck and just drive until he met the horizon. He'd failed a lot of people when he left.

Just like his father.

He shook off the thought through sheer force of will and climbed up into his truck. Jules apparently lived over that shop of hers, and so it took him ten minutes from leaving his mama's house to pulling into the parking lot. Devil's Falls was like that, though. It took fifteen minutes to drive from one end of the town limits to the other—and that was only because of the twenty-mile-an-hour speed limit and single stoplight.

He got out of his truck and looked up and down Main Street. There were the same two bars down the street, the same diner, the same hardware store, the same *everything*. Nothing had changed—not even a fresh coat of paint. The only difference between the street now and when he was eighteen was the addition of a Starbucks down by the stoplight and the café in front of him that used to be a pizza joint.

Restlessness hit him, fierce enough to have him clenching his fists. It wouldn't take much to get back in his truck and keep driving, to search out the nearest rodeo and put in his registration. Everyone in Texas knew him. They'd get him in. He could be on the back of a bull inside of two days. Then maybe he wouldn't have to think about the circles beneath his mama's eyes or the worried looks Lenora kept shooting her when she thought neither of them was watching.

No. You promised you'd stay, and that's what you're going to do.

Adam paused to take in Cups and Kittens again. It was such a random-ass idea—a coffee shop where people could come and spend time with cats—but it was obvious that it was something Jules felt passionately about. Hell, he'd spent a grand total of twenty minutes with her and he could tell that wasn't the only thing.

Judging from that kiss, she was passionate about quite a few things. Just thinking about it calmed the impulse to get the hell out of town. He could do this. The distraction Jules offered pretty much guaranteed he could do this.

It's just a matter of figuring out how far you want to take it.

Now that was a dumb thing to think. He knew exactly how far he wanted to go with Jules Rodriguez.

All the goddamn way.

Adam shook his head, damning himself to hell for the kind of thoughts that type of thing brought up. Her wrapping those long legs around his waist, her mouth on his, her making helpless little noises while he… "Get a hold of yourself. You're not sleeping with the woman. You're taking her on a date." She was a good girl—and Daniel's cousin.

But she wants to be bad.

He ignored the voice inside him and marched around

back to the door where she'd told him to meet her. He barely got his hand up to knock when it was flung open, revealing a breathless Jules. She must have run down the narrow stairs behind her, because her cheeks were flushed and her chest rose and fell hard enough that it looked like her breasts were in danger of spilling free.

Adam nearly swallowed his tongue. "What in the hell are you wearing?"

She looked panicked. "Oh, this little thing?" She pulled at the bottom of her tied-up tank top, belying her attempt at being casual. Not that he was complaining, exactly, but the shorts were several precious inches shorter than the ones she'd worn the other night—so short that the pockets peeked out in the front and he was pretty damn sure if she turned around, he'd be able to see the bottom curve of her ass.

She looked like some country-music video piece of tail.

The only thing that was the same was the well-worn boots on her feet. Jules pushed her mass of dark hair off her face and frowned. "Is something wrong? You said we were going out to burgers, so I didn't dress up and—"

Fuck, she was killing him. "It's fine." But the slice of stomach and length of her long legs and the cleavage that her low-cut tank top revealed...they were making it hard to remember that he was supposed to keep his hands to himself when they weren't in public *trying* to make a spectacle of themselves. *It's still Jules beneath the clothes—what little of them there are.* Right. He just had to remember that, and—

Adam's thoughts screeched to a halt as she turned around and bent over to pick up her purse on the bottom stair. He'd been right about the shorts playing peekaboo with her ass. He gripped the doorframe, unable to tear his gaze away from the place where her mile-long legs met the curve of her ass. The shorts didn't reveal as much as he'd expected, but somehow that only made them more erotic. He wanted to set his teeth to that curve and then lick his way around…

Stop it. For fuck's sake, if you don't, you're going to maul her right here in her doorway.

He forced himself to take a step back, and then another one. She hadn't signed on for hot and sweaty sex, and he had to remember that. This wasn't about him and his nearly unbearable desire for her—as unexpected as it was inconvenient. This was about doing her a favor.

Right. Keep telling yourself that. You wanted a distraction, now don't going complaining that you got what you asked for—in spades.

She locked the door behind her and turned with a smile. "I feel ridiculous. Do I look ridiculous?"

He had to clear his throat twice to answer. "No."

"Are you okay?" Just like that, her smile disappeared, and her face fell. "Oh God, you're lying, aren't you? I look like a two-bit hooker." She pulled on the bottom of her shorts. "I'm going to go change. This was such a bad idea. Maybe we should just call the whole thing off."

"Sugar, stop." He grabbed her wrist, changing her course so that her momentum brought her slamming into his chest. "You look great."

"You're really sweet for lying, but—"

"Jules, stop talking." He pressed his free hand to the small of her back, bringing her flush against him. Her mouth opened in a little O of surprise when she pressed against where he was rock hard. "You feel that?" As if there was any chance of her missing it with them this close. Adam waited for her to nod. "You did that to me. I see you in those little shorts and all I can think of is getting a handful of your ass as I lift you up and thrust against where you're warm and soft and wet for me."

She blinked. "Oh."

It was hard to get himself leashed, harder than it should have been, but he finally managed to take a step back and put some distance between them. "Any questions?"

"Just one." She licked her lips. "Can you teach me to do that?"

He opened the passenger door for her. "Do what?"

"Dirty talk." She hopped up into the seat, giving him another devastating flash of her ass.

He shut the door, buying some time as he walked around the front of the truck and climbed inside. Unfortunately, he hadn't gotten himself back under control by that point. "You want me to teach you to dirty talk."

"It's just…" She waved a hand at him. She'd recovered a whole hell of a lot faster than he had. Adam was almost insulted by how unaffected she seemed. Jules must have finally got her thoughts in order, because she finished, "It's really, really hot. And naughty, though I'm not sure if calling it naughty completely cancels out the hotness factor."

Hearing the word "naughty" on her lips was almost enough to have him pulling over so he could start lesson one. Instead, he gripped the steering wheel and focused on driving. "Yeah, sugar. I can teach you to talk dirty."

Though he was already starting to regret agreeing to this in the first place.

Chapter Five

Jules couldn't quite get her heartbeat under control. She'd hoped she didn't look like an idiot when she dug down to the bottom of her closet to get the not-approved-for-public-consumption clothes. She hadn't expected to watch Adam's eyes go dark or for his voice to drop a full octave when he said...those things. She shivered, staring out the passenger window.

There was no room in her world for wanting Adam Meyer. This was a business arrangement, plain and simple.

It just happened to be a business arrangement where she was having the sudden desire to see if her partner could follow through on the picture he'd painted with his words.

Teach me to dirty talk. Jules almost snorted. That was the most pathetic comeback she'd ever made, but she'd been half a second from kissing him again, and one sexual ambush was more than enough in a lifetime, let alone a week.

I want to create a scandal, but not too *much of a scandal. And only when there are people to watch. Because that totally makes sense.*

She realized they'd be sitting in silence for entirely too long and turned to face Adam. *Might as well own it.* "So, when's my first lesson?"

"I'll let you know."

She wilted a little but managed to get a hold of herself. Of course he wasn't going to start dirty talk lessons in the car on the way to their first fake date. There were a grand total of three restaurants in town, not counting the McDonald's that no one but teenagers and moms of little kids went to, and the Joint was where people tended to congregate on Saturday night before they wandered down the street to the bar or drove off into the boonies for a bonfire.

That was Devil's Falls, though. She liked it, no matter that people like Grant and Adam no doubt looked down on the locals—probably the only thing those two had in common. It was nice to know that on any given weekend night, she could walk down the street and find a few of her uncles or cousins playing poker at the bar, or some of the girls from her graduating class having a ladies' night out at the Joint with classy martinis and cosmos.

But…there was no way she'd be able to walk through the doors of any place in town without running into half a dozen people she knew. Something she hadn't really thought about when she'd gotten dressed. Crap.

That's the whole point of this. To prove you're not a spinster pining after Grant. You're alive and exciting and dating the town bad boy.

If that wasn't scandalous, she didn't know what was.

It sounded great—in theory. In practice, she wasn't sure she'd survive the embarrassment. "Are you sure I don't look ridiculous?" Her shorts were so short, they might be illegal. She pulled at the hem, but it didn't do a single thing to cover her more.

"You look…like a scandal waiting to happen."

She glanced at him, shocked all over again by the edge in his voice. She wasn't sure if he sounded mad or turned on. "Are you okay? If you're not feeling well, we can reschedule for another night."

"Holy fuck." Adam laughed harshly and pulled the truck onto the edge of the road. He turned to her, his shoulders filling the space between the steering wheel and the seat, suddenly seeming a whole lot closer. "Sugar, you're killing me. You're seducing me without even realizing you're doing it."

"I…am?" She realized what she'd said and lifted her chin. "I mean, I am. Good. Right?" She groaned and slouched in her seat. "I'm pretty sure you're not feeling seduced anymore."

She expected him to laugh or something, but he just reached across the bench seat and snagged her waist, dragging her toward him. She bit back a yelp when he lifted her to straddle him. "Uh, I'm pretty sure we're breaking some sort of law right now."

"Nah. We're parked and inside my vehicle. You're covered."

She twisted enough to look through the windshield. There didn't seem to be anyone around, but that didn't mean there weren't eyes on them.

Which is the freaking point. Get it together, girl.

His hands drifted over her hips, not touching so much as a sliver of bare skin, but she felt branded all the same. Was this guy hiding a forest fire beneath his skin? Adam looked at her with those too-dark eyes, his expression serious and yet somehow savage. "Are you ready to make a scene, sugar?"

She licked her lips. *Definitely not a mild-mannered nice guy—more like a lone wolf who's just as likely to cuddle you as rip your throat out.* "Yes. Public display of affection without possibility of arrest. Good thinking."

He smiled. "I'm not going to do anything you don't want me to. You say the word and I stop. Repeat that back to me."

Her heart was beating too fast, her tight clothing seeming to become even tighter with each breath. "You're not going to do anything I don't want you to."

"And?"

"I say the word and you stop." It was harder to get the last part out, mostly because she couldn't stop staring at his mouth. He'd blown her away with the rushed fake kiss the other night. How much better would it be if he was planning on actually, say, kissing her? Her body broke out in goose bumps at the thought. "Adam—"

One of his hands left her hip to frame her jaw, his thumb tracing over her bottom lip. "Rule number one to making this believable—stop overthinking and worrying about who could be watching. Just focus on me and feel."

Easier said than done. "I'm really good at overthinking." Though it was really hard to connect her thoughts with him touching her like that, his thumb coasting back and forth, back and forth.

"I can see that." His fingers curled around the back of her neck, easing her forward. "What are you thinking about now?"

She was forced to brace her hands on his chest to avoid toppling against him, and the feel of all those muscles beneath his T-shirt made her brain short out. She kneaded her fingers, moving up to his shoulders and then down again. Belatedly, she realized he'd asked her something. "I'm sorry, what?"

"That answers that." His hand on her hip tightened. "I'm going to kiss you now."

"Oh…okay."

"That wasn't a request, sugar."

And then he did exactly what he promised he would.

He kept it light, the slightest brushing of his lips on hers, over and over again, until she thought she might go mad with desire. She writhed against him, but he easily held her in place, taking his time, almost as if he was savoring the contact. Then, *finally*, his tongue coaxed her mouth open and he was *kissing* her.

Just like that, the spark between them went from campfire to wild blaze, flaring out of control.

One second she was wondering how in God's name one man could taste so good, and the next she was rubbing against him like he was the best kind of catnip. He groaned against her mouth, his hand on her hip moving to her behind, lining them up. The feel of his hard length against the most sensitive part of her had her going still, but only for a moment. She rolled her hips, moaning at the delicious friction.

Adam took his mouth off hers long enough to curse, long and hard, and then she was on her back on the bench seat, him moving over her, his mouth reclaiming hers. Jules wrapped her legs around his waist, arching up to meet each thrust that dragged him against the seam of her jeans. He kissed down her jaw to her breasts. "Fuck, sugar, you're one hell of an actress."

She laughed, but the sound choked off when he yanked down her tank top and sucked her nipple into his mouth. "Oh my *God*."

For some reason, that caused him to pause. He rested his forehead against her chest. "Hold on. Give me a second."

That sounded dangerously close to him saying he wanted to stop. She grabbed his shoulders, digging her nails in. "Adam, I'm three seconds from coming. If you don't finish what you started…" She couldn't think of a threat strong enough, so she just made an incoherent sound of frustration. When he didn't immediately move, she actually whimpered. "Please, Adam. Remember what you said? I'll let you know when to stop. Well, I don't know how else to tell you to keep going. Full steam ahead. Green light. *Just make me come already.*"

His body shook, and it took her a full two seconds to

realize he was laughing. "You are something else."

"As long as I'm something else that will be coming in short order." Never in her life had she been this *forward* with anything sexual, but she felt like she might burst apart at the seams if he didn't answer the beat pulsing through her body.

It was easier to demand it because this was Adam. He wasn't her boyfriend, no matter what they were pretending. He wasn't even a friend, really. He was just a seriously sexy guy doing her a favor that might nominate him for sainthood. She gasped when he grabbed her butt, sealing their bodies together. *Okay, maybe not sainthood.*

"Just this once."

She wasn't sure she could handle more than once. "Sure. Whatever you say." *As long as you don't stop.*

He hooked her leg higher and thrust against her, building up to the rhythm that had driven her so crazy. His mouth was on her neck, his words pouring over her. "I lied, sugar. I make you come once, and I don't think I'm going to be able to stop myself from doing it again. It's what a good boyfriend would do."

"Fake…boyfriend." She could barely get the words out past the pleasure spiking through her. Her orgasm rolled over her, setting her nerves aflame and making her entire body go tight and hot. "*Holy crap.*"

His laugh was almost a growl against her skin. "A fake boyfriend who gives you real orgasms." He held her for a few seconds, long enough for her to realize he was still hard as a rock. Adam didn't give her a chance to comment on it, though. He sat back and adjusted his jeans, leaving her to do the same.

Jules fixed her clothing, feeling like she was having an out-of-body experience. Had she really just dry humped her fake boyfriend in his pickup until he made her come? She had to say something, right now, otherwise they were going to devolve into what might be the most awkward situation of her life. She cleared her throat and looked around. "Oh, wow, this was a good call. I see Sheriff Taylor's police cruiser down the road. He saw something for sure, and he gossips worse than Mrs. Peterson."

There was a pause. And then finally, "Yep. That was the plan."

The words came out flat, and she twisted to look at him. "Are you okay? I'm sorry that I basically just strong-armed you into giving me an orgasm." Humiliation rolled over her despite her determination to push herself beyond her limits. "You tried to stop and I said no and, oh my God, I'm so sorry."

Adam turned to face her again. "Sugar, you couldn't have forced me if you wanted to." He grabbed her hand and pressed it to the front of his jeans, where it was still blatantly obvious that he was sporting an erection. "Don't you dare try to take that orgasm from me. It was mine."

She stared at his lap, not quite having the courage to stroke him despite the fact her palm was plastered there. "I, uh…"

"If it makes you feel better, next time I'll be the one giving the orders."

Next time. She blinked up at him. "You really weren't joking about making this as believable as possible, were you?"

His mouth flattened, but then Adam smiled and she was sure she'd misread the expression. "I never joke about fake relationships."

"Hilarious." She realized she was still palming him and yanked her hand back. "But, seriously, you have to stop me when I'm out of line. I know we were just doing it for show but—"

"Sugar, stop. Remember what I said about overthinking? You're doing it again. Sit back and relax, and let the rumor mill do its job." Before she could answer, he pulled away from the side of the road, and, two minutes later, they were in the parking lot and he shut off the engine. "Brace yourself. It's showtime."

Chapter Six

Adam was having a hell of a time focusing on what Jules was saying. She was obviously really passionate about it, which was making him think of what *else* she'd be passionate about. Again. Every time she smiled, his cock jumped, reminding him that he hadn't gotten the same release she'd so obviously enjoyed back in the cab of his truck.

For fuck's sake, focus.

"…but I'm boring you. I'm so sorry."

He blinked. "What?"

"I'm prattling on and you'd obviously rather be anywhere else but here." Her self-deprecating smile tugged at him. "I don't get out much, and the stuff I talk about with Aubry isn't exactly fit for polite company, and when I get nervous, I start rambling and, seriously, just tell me to shut up right now or I'm going to keep going."

"Jules, breathe."

She took a gasping breath. "Right. Sorry again."

The woman was downright precious. He pushed his plate away and sat back. "When's the last time you were on a date?"

"Does the charity auction count?" She tugged on her tank top, which only served to make it dip dangerously. "What am I saying? Of course it doesn't count. The only reason Dave went out with me was because I donated money to the PTA, and really, he kissed like a drowning fish, so it was never going to be anything more than one dinner."

Adam took a sip of his beer, picking over what she just said. "They still do that charity auction for the high school?"

"Every year like clockwork." She made a face. "As fun as it is, I can almost tell who's going to bid on who, though there's always at least one upset every year. Last year, Mrs. Peterson bid *three hundred dollars* on Sheriff Taylor. His wife wasn't very happy about that."

Considering Mrs. Taylor was one of the scariest women he'd ever met, Mrs. Peterson had balls of steel to pull that one off. But then, he'd known that in eighth grade, when she was his English teacher. She didn't take any shit then, and apparently that hadn't changed in the years since. "So, back to your date."

"It was fine." She picked up her fork, poked at her salad, and set it down again. For once, he wasn't the twitchiest person in the room, and he was content to watch her fidget. She used her straw to stir the ice in her water, not looking at him, her head dipped so that her dark hair fell forward to hide her face.

He waited, but she didn't say anything else, and since she was managing to look everywhere but at him, he figured she wasn't going to. "Talk about damning with faint praise."

"It was for *charity*." She slumped in her chair and sighed. "It's obvious I don't get out much, isn't it? No wonder the whole town thinks I'm a lonely cat-collecting spinster."

She was so cute, it was downright painful. He just wanted to scoop her up and tell her that her adorable awkwardness was an asset—not something to be ashamed of. To hell with what the town thought. She was fresh and enthusiastic and as bracing as a dive into a mountain lake.

Adam shook his head and finished off his beer. If he was any other man, he'd tell her to forget her preoccupation with Grant. She didn't need to fake date him in order to make a point—she was doing just fine on her own.

But he wasn't any other man, and he had no intention of leaving her alone.

He held the door open for Jules and followed her out into the night. *Just get her home without mauling her again and then you can figure out what your next step is.* He couldn't call the whole thing off. Now that half the town had either seen them at dinner or likely heard about it, them "breaking up" would only add a heap of humiliation on Jules's already teetering pile, and Adam refused to contribute. She'd asked him for a favor, and it wasn't her fault that his control was slipping by the second.

She climbed into his truck, seeming preoccupied with something. That was fine. If they managed to keep silent for the whole five-minute drive, it would be all good.

But then she went and shot that plan all to hell. "I think tonight went okay."

"Yep."

"I mean, Grant wasn't there, but from the stares we got, he'll be hearing about our being seen together before too long. *Everyone* will be hearing about it." She sounded pleased, which was good. So why did it grate against him as badly now as it had back in the truck? She continued, oblivious to his inner aggravation. "What's next?"

Did she think he kept a copy of *Idiot's Guide to Being a Small-Town Scandal* stuffed in his dresser drawer? Apparently so, because she was looking at him expectantly. He turned out on Main Street. "Sugar, we already made spectacles of ourselves nearly getting busy in my truck with Sheriff Taylor half a block away, then proceeded to shock the locals just by eating dinner. Why don't we take it easy for the rest of the night?"

"I don't know." She frowned. "Shouldn't we be taking it to the next level? We don't know for sure the sheriff saw anything."

Frankly, he doubted the old man had seen anything. Adam knew for a fact Sheriff Taylor liked to nap on that very side street around that time of night, and so he wouldn't have had his glasses on. But he sure as fuck wasn't going to tell Jules that. "Are you asking me or telling me?"

She laughed. "Sorry. I haven't spent much time thinking about indulging in gossip-starting acts. The craziest I get these days is video games. I'm a halfway decent sniper."

The woman just kept surprising him. "I never would have pegged you for a first-person shooter."

"Oh, not by my own doing." She grinned. "But they're Aubry's poison of choice, so I get dragged along when she starts annihilating noobs."

Now, the redhead he could picture camped out in a dark room with a microphone on her head and a controller in her hands. She was as intense as Jules was sunny. In fact, despite being around them a grand total of an hour, he couldn't really wrap his mind around how they were friends. "How did you and Aubry meet?"

"It's a silly story."

"Humor me."

"If you insist." She turned, fully engaged. Jules seemed to spend her entire life fully engaged. "So my grandmother passed when I was a junior in college. I already knew what I wanted to do for a career—start a coffee shop with a unique draw—and she left me enough money to get off the ground, plus her blessing along with it." She smiled, her eyes going soft. "Gran was one of the few people in town—my family included—who didn't think I'd end up a lonely spinster after Grant dumped me."

Before he could comment that he thought it highly unlikely Jules would hit thirty and still be single, let alone a spinster, she continued on, "So I'd just bought and renovated the shop, and I was down at the Humane Society picking the cats that would live there. Aubry was carting her massive laptop home from the library and saw me loading what she termed 'a cat lady's starter kit' into my truck. She made some comment about cats eating you after you die, and of course I couldn't let that stand. We ended up arguing all the way back to my place and while she helped me unload the cats and get them settled. From there it's more or less history. Aubry has her quirks, same as me, and she doesn't expect me to be something I'm not."

Friends like that were worth their weight in gold. He'd had three, now two, and he'd barely seen them over the last twelve years. *I'm a leaver, just like my mama always said.* Once upon a time, those words had been a promise—Devil's Falls and its whispers and judgment wouldn't hold him back forever—but now they felt more like a curse.

He turned into the alley leading to the little carport behind Jules's shop. "And what's she think about this plan you've concocted?"

"She thinks I'm crazy." Jules laughed again. "But then, she tells me I'm crazy at least once a day, so that's nothing new."

He parked but hesitated turning off the engine. It was all too easy to step back to the last time they'd been in his truck cab and the trouble he'd let them get into. Adam gripped the steering wheel, reminding himself for the dozenth time that he sure as hell could *not* kiss Jules again.

She took the decision right out of his hands. "See you later." She dashed a quick kiss against his cheek and bounced away, opening the door and sliding out of the truck before he could respond.

Adam watched her bound to her door and let herself in, her enthusiasm infectious even over the distance. He finally shook his head and threw his truck into reverse.

Aubry was right—Jules was bat-shit crazy.

And he loved it.

Shit.

• • •

Five days passed with only a few texts from Adam, but Jules told herself she didn't care. He had his own life to attend to, just like she did. She couldn't expect him to drop everything to spend every minute of every day by her side on the off chance that Grant would wander in and see them.

Coincidentally, her ex had made a habit of waltzing through the door at least once a day to make comments about her *boyfriend* in such a tone that she knew he still didn't believe she was with Adam.

She took the plate of sandwiches Jamie had made up special and brought them over to where Lenora and Amelia were sitting at a table by the window. Lenora smiled in thanks, but Jules couldn't help noticing that Adam's mom had lost weight. "These are on the house."

"Oh, Jules, you shouldn't have." Amelia sipped her tea, petting Rick.

Lenora sent her a look of thanks. "I know you just said you're not hungry, but you can't let this go to waste," she said to Amelia.

"Let me know if you need anything else."

She headed back to the counter, leaving the ladies in peace.

But they were apparently the only ones going to be left in peace today. As if her wishing him ill conjured him up, the bell above the door jingled and Grant strode through. "Jules!" He stopped just inside the door and examined the floor at his feet. He had this nasty habit of looking around him like he expected to step in cat shit, which made Jules grind her teeth every time she saw it.

"Grant."

"Douchecanoe," Aubry muttered from her usual place in the corner. Jules shot her a sharp look, but she appeared engrossed in whatever she was doing on her computer.

Grant came up and leaned on the counter but immediately backpedaled when Cujo hissed at him. "That thing's rabid."

"He doesn't like people." She crossed her arms over her chest. "Are you buying something today?"

"Nope. There's a double Frappuccino down the street with my name on it. I was just stopping in to see if you and your *boyfriend* were going to the swimming hole tomorrow for the Fourth?"

"For fuck's sake, you can't be serious." Aubry leaned back, stretching her arms over her head. "Going to the swimming hole is something high school kids who can't legally drink do. I'm pretty sure that'd look great on your future law résumé."

Grant's mouth tightened, his gray eyes going flinty. But then he turned back to Jules, the expression melting into a charming smile she used to believe was real. "There will be a bunch of people from our class there. You should come. Bring Adam." He jerked a thumb over his shoulder at Aubry. "You can even bring her."

"She has a name."

His smile never wavered. "Of course. I'd be delighted if you'd come and bring your boyfriend and *Aubry*." He made a show of looking around. "Unless Adam's already blown out of town? It's been over a week, and word has it that he's more tumbleweed than man."

She opened her mouth to deny it, but that would be a lie.

Fake relationship or not, she couldn't pretend like Adam was staying for the long term. "Actually —"

"Hey, there, sugar."

Jules nearly jumped out of her skin when Adam walked in from the door to the kitchen, his damned eyebrow inching up.

Grant frowned. "Speak of the devil."

"Grant. Aubry." He slipped an arm around Jules's waist. "Jules." He kissed her forehead, the innocent touch doing some very *non*innocent things to her lower stomach area.

"Hey." She turned in his arms and wrapped hers around his neck. "I've missed you."

"Not nearly much as I've missed you." He grabbed her ass, making her squeal, and turned to Grant. "What are *you* doing here? I know for a fact you get your coffee needs met at that abomination down the street."

For his part, her ex recovered remarkably fast. "I was just stopping by to invite Jules here to the swimming hole this weekend. You're welcome to come, of course."

"Wouldn't miss it." He didn't take his gaze off the other man, something dangerous glinting in his eyes. "If you're done here…"

"Yeah. Sure. I'll be going." Grant strode out of the shop at a clip almost fast enough to be called running.

"You made the puppy piddle his pants. That was mean." Aubry snickered. "I like it."

"So glad you approve." He combed a hand over Cujo's back, and Jules's mouth dropped open when the tabby arched into his hand, purring like a jet engine. His gaze traveled around the café and landed on where his mom and Lenora were watching avidly. "You ladies like the show?"

Amelia laughed. "I always thought that boy was a brat."

A brat. Well, that was one way to describe Grant.

Adam eyed the uneaten sandwiches on the plate between

them. "You eat some of that, you hear? You're too skinny by half."

She arched a brow, the expression so similar to her son's that Jules had to bite back a laugh. "I was just getting to it before you started that prize cock show."

"Mama."

"What? I'm old, but I'm not dead. I know exactly what you were up to." When he turned back to Jules, Amelia leaned over and sent her a wink.

He sure does love his mama. It made her like him even better knowing that.

Adam leaned against the counter, giving Cujo another stroke. "So Grant wants us to come to the swimming hole?"

She ignored Aubry's muttered agreement. "I get the impression Grant still doesn't believe the rumors that we're together."

"Then I guess we'll just have to kick it up a notch." His grin did funny things to her stomach, and her traitorous mind jumped back to what he'd said before their date the other night, and how good he'd felt when he made her come.

She pressed a hand to her flaming cheeks, hating that he made her blush so easily. "I guess I'm going to have to find a swimsuit."

He blinked. "You don't own a swimsuit?"

"Well, I do. But, you see—"

"What Jules is trying to say is that to describe her suit as 'matronly' would be to put it kindly."

"Aubry, shut up," she hissed, blushing even harder when Adam laughed. "You shut up, too. There's nothing wrong with wanting a suit that will keep all my goodies in place no matter how I'm moving."

His hands skated up her sides and back down to her hips. "Do you need some help picking out a suit?"

Danger! It was all too easy to imagine the kind of trouble they could get into in a fitting room with her scantily clad in a bathing suit. "Uh, no, thanks. Aubry will help me."

She might have imagined the disappointment that flickered over his face, but it was gone too fast to be sure. "In that case, I'll pick you up at eleven tomorrow."

"How do you know what time they're going?"

"Because it's a party at the swimming hole. They always start at noon." He hesitated, almost like he thought he should kiss her good-bye or something, but then he seemed to think better of it, because he turned on his heel and marched back through the door to the kitchen.

It took Jules a few seconds to get control of her body enough to follow him. "Hey, hold up!" She caught him just inside the door out to the back parking lot. "Why'd you come in this way?" *And what are you doing here in the first place?*

"I've been working on my mama's place, so I was picking up a few things at the hardware store across the street and saw that jackass walk in here. Figured it was a good time to remind him of our fake relationship."

"Oh." She had no business feeling the disappointment that made her stomach dip. He was doing her a favor. That was it. "That's smart."

"Hang in there. He might not believe yet, but he will after by the time we leave that party." And then he was gone, disappearing through the door and leaving her to wonder if she should be looking forward to tomorrow or scared out of her godforsaken mind.

Chapter Seven

"I thought only high school kids did this shit."

Adam unhooked the last black tube and tossed it into the back of his truck. "They do. But I get the feeling Grant is trying to recapture his glory days." *And maybe Jules, too.*

Quinn snorted. "The more I hear about this guy, the more he sounds like a winner." He looked around. "Where's Daniel?"

"He's busy." Or, more likely, he didn't want to see his cousin and Adam putting on a show for a guy he hated. Adam was sorry he felt that way, but he'd seen the look on Jules's face when he walked into her shop today. Grant got under her skin in a bad way, and watching the light in her eyes dim had grated on Adam something fierce. There was enough bad shit in this world without that asshat making her feel like she was lacking.

Adam wasn't exactly a white knight, though. He was taking advantage of her with these "lessons."

Which made him no better than Grant, in the end.

Adam looked at his hands. He had calluses across his

palms from rope burns, and there was the scar on his right ring finger where he'd broken it in a truly impressive way after being thrown from a bull with the name of Satan's Revenge. He'd only managed four seconds that ride, but it had been more than worth it.

What he wouldn't give to take it back and know he'd been by his mama's side when she found out about the cancer instead.

"You okay?"

He blinked. "What?"

Quinn looked distinctly uncomfortable to be shucking aside the joking demeanor he preferred. "I don't know, man. You just seem kind of lost since you got back into town. Is it your mom? I know she's sick—"

"She's fine." He wasn't ready to admit that she wouldn't even talk about the cancer with him. Not now, not like this. There would come a time when he'd have to sit her down and force it out of her, but he sure as fuck wasn't ready for it yet. Really, he should thank Jules. When they were together, he was able to forget his fear that one day he'd wake up and his mama would be gone for good.

He realized he'd spoken too sharply and sighed. "Look, it's complicated and I'm not handling it well."

"No shit." Quinn hesitated. "If you need anything— anything at all—I'm here. You know that, right?"

"Yeah."

"And Daniel is, too, even if he's got his own shit he's dealing with." He held up a hand before Adam could ask. "It's the same old, same old. He was never the same after John died and Hope left. The man has one foot in the grave, and it's by choice."

The car crash affected them all. Everything changed after that night, and little of it for the better. Adam wished there was something he could do for Daniel, but the truth was that he had more than enough shit to deal with on his own. *Fuck.* He swiped a beer from the cooler in the back of the truck and opened it. "What a trio we make."

"Speak for yourself. I'm the normal one."

Quinn was as normal as he could be after having walked away from his oil tycoon of a father—and his family's fortune—to be a cattle rancher. Adam shook his head. "Whatever you have to tell yourself to sleep at night."

"Like a baby." Quinn closed the tailgate. "So is that mean little redhead coming?"

"Don't know. She doesn't seem like the type to be into this sort of thing."

"You mean she's like a vampire who'll burn up in the sun and probably feasts on the blood of innocents? I totally agree."

Adam snorted. "You enjoy pushing her buttons."

"More than I should." He laughed. "I can't help it. It's too easy to get a rise out of her."

"Get your ass in the truck or we're going to be late."

Ten minutes later they pulled up in front of Jules's shop. He stopped the truck and froze when Jules and Aubry stepped through the door and onto the sidewalk. "Holy fucking shit."

"You can say that again."

"Shut up." He couldn't take his eyes off Jules. She wore a pair of cutoff shorts that might've been the same ones from the other night, but this time, there were ties peeking out the top on either side of her hips. It was like seeing the tip of a present he was dying to unwrap. Adam's cock jumped to attention as his gaze coasted up her stomach to the tiny black triangle bikini covering her breasts. There was nothing overtly revealing about the cut of the suit, but it had him fighting not to kick Quinn out of the truck and drive her off to somewhere they wouldn't be interrupted so he could explore those scraps of cloth at length.

"Jesus, man. If you could see the way you're looking at her." Quinn shook his head. "Should I get another ride?"

"What? No. It's fine." Though he wanted to tell his friend to do exactly that. *Get a hold of yourself, idiot.* He had to control himself—he was about to be up close and personal with Jules, and jumping her bones the second he saw her wasn't acceptable.

"Sure it is." Quinn hopped out of the truck, and Adam took several deep breaths and focused on getting his body's reaction minimized. He didn't have long, because Jules climbed up and scooted over until she was pressed against him from shoulder to hip, Aubry on the other side of her.

Quinn wedged his big body into the tiny space between the redhead and the door. "There's plenty of room for you right here, sweet cheeks." He patted his lap.

She shot him a look that would have sent a lesser man bolting from the truck. "Touch me and lose the attached body part."

Quinn just grinned. "You're all sugar and spice and everything nice, aren't you?"

Hearing the redhead's hiss of rage was almost enough to distract Adam from how good Jules smelled—like coconut and suntan lotion. He smiled at her. "You ready for this?"

"Not in the least." Her eyes were a little too wide. "It's bringing back all sorts of memories I could do without."

Memories of her and Grant. The thought sent a completely irrational spike of jealousy through him. That shit had gone down years ago. There was no reason for him to want to wring the man's neck for knowing that he'd once gotten to touch Jules whenever he wanted, or that he'd held her heart close enough to break it.

Or, hell, that he still affected her strongly enough nine years later that she was willing to get up close and personal with a near stranger to prove a point.

Adam turned back to the road, clenching his jaw to keep words inside that he had no right to. He didn't have *any* rights when it came to Jules, and it'd do him good to remember that.

The rest of the trip up was done in painful silence. He was almost grateful for the fact that Aubry had taken an instant dislike to Quinn's poking at her, because her icy one-word answers to him made conversation between Adam and Jules damn near impossible. He parked next to two other trucks. Of the two, he pegged the shiny pavement queen to be Grant's—the red Ford must have had all of ten miles on the engine. His ten-year-old Dodge looked battered and beaten by comparison.

He'd be an idiot not to see the similarities between the trucks and their owners.

It was enough to give a lesser man a complex.

Adam got out of the cab before anyone could say something to tip him over the edge and strode around to the back to start unpacking the tubes.

"Is everything okay?"

He didn't look over at Jules. "I could live the rest of my life happy knowing I wouldn't hear that question again from another damn person."

If he expected her to rabbit away from his snarled words, he was sadly mistaken. "You don't have to do this. We can just say something came up and skip it."

Even if he was willing to do that—and piss-poor mood or not, he couldn't let Jules down so spectacularly—the chance to bolt disappeared when Grant came around the back of the truck and waved. "I'm glad you made it." He did a double take when he saw Jules. "I can't believe your mama let you out of the door dressed like that."

She narrowed her eyes. "Funny thing—I have my own place, and I'm not sixteen anymore."

"I can see that." And then he proceeded to rake her with

his gaze in a way that had Adam seeing red. He stalked over to slip an arm around her waist, telling himself all the while that he was playing a part.

It sure as fuck didn't *feel* like a part. It felt like he was half a second from beating that smug piece of shit's face in. Adam put every ounce of that desire onto his face when he clenched his teeth in a way that only a fool would call a grin. "Didn't your daddy ever teach you that it's not nice to eye-fuck another man's woman, let alone when he's standing not two feet away?"

Grant took a step back and seemed to catch himself because he straightened, his shoulders going back. "You know as well as I do that she's not the kind of—"

"Boy, I suggest you rethink the words that are about to come out of your idiot mouth."

Grant's teeth clicked together when he snapped his mouth shut. He glared. "Hurry up. The party's already started." Then he strode away, yanking his shirt off and pausing to shove it into his truck before he disappeared down the path leading to the swimming hole.

"Well, that was…" Jules let out a shuddering breath. "I'm sorry I got you into this."

"I offered to keep this thing going, remember? You didn't get me into anything I didn't want to do." He forced the tension out of his body. He'd wanted to do this because Jules offered a one-of-a-kind distraction from the shit his mom was going through, but that didn't do a damn thing if he didn't *let* her distract him. "I'm just in a piss-poor mood, and it has nothing to do with you."

"Okay." She didn't sound sure, though. But she brightened immediately. "I'll grab the beer."

He was quickly learning that Jules covered up nearly any uncomfortable emotion with cheer. It should have been annoying as fuck, but it was strangely endearing. Then she shimmied out of her shorts and he forgot about everything but the fact her heart-shaped ass was barely covered by her bikini bottom.

He rubbed a hand over his face, his chances of making it through the day without killing Grant Thomas—or fucking Jules senseless—disappearing before his eyes.

Chapter Eight

Jules could feel Adam's eyes on her, and it was driving her crazy. She tried to focus on where Aubry floated next to her, her friend's giant hat shielding her face and chest, and her equally giant sunglasses masking any expression of judgment that she was sure to be leveling at Jules right about now. "Sorry."

"You keep saying that. I keep not believing you. In fact, I don't think that word means what you think it means." She held her hand out, and Jules passed her another beer from the cooler strung between Jules and Adam's tubes. Aubry took a long drink and sank lower into the hole in the middle of her tube. "But it could be worse."

"Dear God, was that an actual admission of you having fun doing something outside surrounded by *nature*?"

Aubry laughed. "Let's not get ahead of ourselves. It's entirely possible that some undiscovered-until-now alligator will appear to pick us off one by one." She seemed to consider. "But if that bastard starts with Grant, I might be okay with my inevitable fate."

She looked over to where Grant floated near them, surrounded by Kelly, Kelli, and Jessica. They were all former cheerleaders, and all were conveniently single and looking to sink their claws into an up-and-coming lawyer.

That's not fair. You were panting after Grant for years.

As if he could read her mind, Grant shot her a look over his shoulder and grinned. "Hope you're having as great a time as I am, Jules."

She gritted out a smile. "Of course. This is just peachy."

"Sugar, you're lying through your teeth." Adam snagged the line between their tubes and towed her closer to him until they squeaked as they rubbed together.

"Only totally." She lowered her voice. "The water's freezing, I'm mostly naked, and now Aubry's got me thinking about mutant alligators. I used to love this, but for the life of me, I can't remember why."

"Is it because of that trio?"

"No." She let her head drop back to rest on her tube. "Yes. Maybe. I don't know. I don't want anything to do with him, but *seeing* him makes me crazy."

It was probably karma kicking her in the lady bits for thinking she could stick it to Grant by doing the same damn thing. She should have taken a page from his book and let him think she had a harem of men stashed away, all ready to drop everything and see to her needs. She laughed at the thought.

"What's so funny?"

She debated not telling him for half as second, but it was too much. Besides, the brisk breeze had eased them just out of earshot of the rest of their group. "Just picturing if Grant's and my positions were reversed and I had three gorgeous men hanging on bated breath for my attention. The imaginary look on his face is very satisfying, if you were wondering."

"I wasn't." Adam put his hand on her knee, the contact shockingly warm. "I'm hurt, sugar. You think one of me isn't man enough for you?"

Jules was suddenly very aware that she was wearing a sad excuse for a swimsuit and that it wouldn't take but a second to divest her of it if Adam was interested. She went very still, torn between wanting to laugh the whole thing off and wanting to take his hand and slide it higher up her thigh. Her skin felt too tight, her nipples pebbling in a way that had nothing to do with temperature. "Oh, no. You're great. I mean, uh, yeah." *You can do better than this.* "So, about that dirty-talking lesson…"

His hand tightened almost imperceptibly. "You want that lesson *now*?"

"No time like the present." It was such a bad idea, but dragging Adam into some of the trees lining the swimming hole was an even worse idea. "How do I start?" She cleared her throat. "Adam, I'd very much like you to stick your bits into my bits."

Adam laughed, the sound deep and carrying. "Holy shit, sugar."

"That's not exactly the reaction I was going for." She frowned and tried again. "I want your c-co… Dang it, I can't say it. Why can't I say it? It's a freaking male chicken."

He tilted his sunglasses down so he could shoot her a look over the top of them. "There isn't a damn thing in common with a male chicken and my cock."

The way he said it, as if it was just another word, inexplicably made her stomach tighten. And his hand was still on her knee. "Fine. I already said I suck at this. Teach me, Master Adam."

"Patience, young padawan." He kneaded the sensitive skin above her knee. "You want to know the trick to dirty talking? It's to say everything with confidence. You don't give the other person enough time or space to stop and think and feel awkward about what they're hearing." His hand inched higher. "Like right now, I want nothing more than to untie one side of that tiny bikini and touch that pretty pussy of yours, spreading you where only I can see you. I'd tease you, sugar, dragging you closer and closer to orgasm. And them?" He jerked his chin at the rest of their party. "They wouldn't have a fucking clue."

Her body felt too hot and too cold, all at the same time. She shifted, pressing her legs together, trapping his hand between them. *This is a lesson. He's not really going to do that...no matter how good of an idea it suddenly sounds like.* She could be student to his teacher without begging him to follow through on his example. Really, she could. "Oh." She took a breath and tried again. "I thought the whole point was that they knew what we were up to."

"Right now, we're focusing on the dirty talking. Now, your turn." His voice deepened. "What would you do to me, sugar?"

I can do this. It was too much to look at him, though, so she leaned back and closed her eyes, the words barely more than a whisper. "After you...make me come..." Her face felt like it was on fire. "It wouldn't be enough. I'd want to return the favor." He made an indecipherable sound, but she kept going because if she stopped now, she wasn't going to start up again. "I'd kiss you. I very much like kissing you, Adam." She licked her lips, almost able to taste him. "And while I was kissing you, I'd, ah, stroke you." *Maybe this isn't so bad.* His hand made rhythmic circles on her skin, relaxing her further. "I'd slip my hand into your shorts and touch you there." She could almost imagine doing exactly this, his hard length filling her hand. "I want to see you go wild and know it's because of me."

"Sugar—"

But she was on a roll. "I think I'd like to give you head."

The only warning she got was him standing and his grip

tightening and then suddenly her world flipped upside down. Jules shrieked, her face barely an inch from the water, her ass in the air. "Adam!"

He didn't answer her as he dragged their tubes to the shore and looped the rope around a half-downed tree. He didn't stop there, though. Adam marched into the trees, not stopping until she could barely hear the faint sounds of their friends talking. Only then did he set her on her feet. She glared. "What the hell?"

"You wanted everyone to know what we're up to? Now's the time." He grabbed her hand and pressed it to the front of his swim trunks.

"That's not…" Her words failed her at the feel of him in her hand, hot and hard through the wet fabric. It felt better than she'd imagined. *Take your hand away. This is supposed to be pretend. Take it away right this second.* But she didn't. Instead, she stroked him lightly. "What are we doing?"

His eyes had gone dark again, turning almost black as he backed her against a tree. "I don't know." And then his mouth was on hers.

She met him halfway, looping one arm around his neck, the other pinned between their bodies. This wasn't pretend. This wasn't even on the same planet as pretend. *This is a mistake.* But the thought was swept away on a tide of desire unlike any she'd ever experienced before. He untied her top and jerked the fabric down, baring her breasts. He kissed his way down to her chest, sucking on first one nipple and then the other, lashing their sensitive tips with his tongue. "Fuck, sugar, I knew I was in trouble the second I saw you in this goddamn excuse for a bikini. So fucking sexy." His hands were gripping her hips so tightly, it was as if he thought she'd float away if he let go. "And then you go and start talking filthy at me…I'm not a goddamn saint. You want a scandal? We're about to create one."

She tangled her fingers into his hair, holding him against her. "If this is what being scandalized feels like, I've been missing out."

"Damn straight." He chuckled against her skin. "I'm going to undo your bottoms right now, sugar. The same rules from the other night apply."

As if she was going to do a single thing to keep him from making her come again. If he could nearly make the top of her head explode while they were both wearing all their clothes, how much better would it be with them naked?

She lifted her hips, a silent invitation he seemed only too happy to accept. Adam met her gaze as he pulled the string loose, letting the fabric slide down her other leg. And then she might as well have been naked. Before reason could reassert why this was a terrible idea, his hand was there between her thighs, a light touch that was more about exploring than domination. He watched her face the entire time as he pushed a single finger into her. The position was almost unbearably intimate, so she closed her eyes, concentrating on the sensations building.

"You like this, don't you, sugar? You like knowing that you drove me so fucking crazy that I carted you out here like a wild man. Every single one of them knows what I'm doing to you, and I don't fucking care. All I can think about is sinking into your wet heat and hearing you come for me again." He pumped his finger in and out of her, slowly, as if savoring every second of it. "I'm going to taste you here, sugar."

She barely had time to process that, and then he was on his knees, lifting her and spreading her thighs, pinning her between his mouth and the tree behind her. He kissed her center the same way he kissed her mouth—as if he owned every part of her. Maybe she'd be worried about that later. Right now all she could do was hang on and try to keep her cries from echoing through the trees around them.

Chapter Nine

Adam was totally and completely out of control, and he didn't give two fucks. He was consumed with driving Jules out of her goddamn mind. He should have known that things would end up this way the second he picked her up. He was so tired of fighting his attraction to her. She obviously wanted him as much as he wanted her.

It's just sex. We can stop anytime we want to.

He'd worry about the fallout later. Right now he had more important things on his mind—Jules's orgasm. He licked and teased and did his damnedest to drive her as crazy as she'd been driving him since he agreed to this devil's bargain. Her whimpers and whispered pleas were music to his ears, and he didn't stop, didn't slow down, didn't so much as change his pace until she gave a muffled cry and her entire body went tight. He gave her one last long lick and then gently set her back onto the ground. "That's how crazy you drive me, sugar."

She blinked down at him. "That's pretty crazy."

"Tell me about it." He climbed to his feet and set about putting her to rights, tying her bikini bottom back into place and reaching for the top.

Jules grabbed his hands. "Wait, what about you?"

"What about me?"

She gave his swim trunks a significant look. "This is the second time you've taken care of me and not gotten your own release."

He knew that. Hell, he could feel every beat of his heart in his cock, and it was as distracting as the fact she was standing here having this conversation with her breasts bared. "Now's not the time." He wasn't sure there ever *would* be a time when it was right, because he didn't trust himself to keep his head on straight, not if he was already reacting this way and he hadn't even been inside her.

"Bullshit."

He frowned at her. "I don't think I've ever heard you swear before."

"There's a time and place. This is both." She swung around, pushing him against the tree with more strength than he would have anticipated. "Now don't even try arguing with me, Adam." Her sunny grin made something in his chest lurch. "I'm about to have my wicked way with you."

"Jules—"

But it was too late. She was on her knees and working off his wet trunks with efficient motions.

You're full of shit. It's not too late. All you have to do is walk away to put a stop to this.

He didn't. He didn't so much as utter a word as she freed his cock, her hum of approval the sexiest thing he'd ever heard. She shot him a look from beneath her lashes. "Now, if you're still having second thoughts, just close your eyes and think of England."

"I'm good." He wanted every second of this memory etched in his brain. Adam laced his fingers through her long dark hair, pulling it away from her face so he could see everything.

"Suit yourself." She took his cock into her mouth, a slow, savoring motion, licking him like he was her favorite kind of ice cream. "Holy wow, Adam—you're packing some serious heat."

There was no appropriate response to that because she took him deeper this time, working him like she had all the time in the world. Watching his cock disappear between her lips did a number on him, the pleasure so intense it was an active fight to keep his eyes open and his body still.

There was no chance of holding his words in. "That's it, sugar. Take me deep. You're making me feel so fucking good I can barely stand it." That earned him a particularly hard suck, and he temporarily lost the ability to breathe. "*Shit.* You're so goddamn lucky I don't have a condom on me, or I'd be on you in half a second, spreading those sweet thighs and sinking into your wet heat. You want that, sugar, don't you?"

She made a sound of agreement, her eyes flashing open to pin him in place.

"Yeah, I thought so. But you deserve better than to be fucked out in the woods like we're horny teenagers. I'm going to take you in a bed, where I can have you in every position imaginable."

She let go of his cock with a wet sound. "Are you taking requests?"

How she could joke in this moment when it felt like he was going to burn to ash on the spot was anyone's guess. He tightened his grip on her hair, not guiding her, just letting her know how close he was to losing it. "I'll consider it."

"I want to be on top."

It was a good thing the tree was holding him up, or his knees would have given out. Adam could perfectly picture what it would be like, her tight little body riding him, her breasts bouncing with each stroke, her dark hair everywhere, her eyes giving him the exact same look she was giving him now—the one that said she was having the time of her life and loving every second of it. "I think we can make that happen."

"Perfect." And then she was back, sucking him deep, working him until he had to let go of her hair with one hand and reach above his head to cling to the nearest tree branch.

"Sugar, if you don't stop what you're doing, I'm going to lose it."

"Good." The word was full of feminine satisfaction. She cupped his balls with one hand, her fingers digging into his hip with the other.

And he was lost. Adam couldn't keep his eyes open, no matter how hard he tried. He came violently, pumping into her mouth with a curse, and she swallowed down every drop. They were silent for several minutes afterward, Jules resting her head on his thigh and him staring up into the treetops and wondering what the fuck he was going to do.

Once again, she recovered faster than he did. Jules patted his thigh. "That was most excellent. They definitely know we were up to no good, and if Kelli can keep it to herself, I'll eat my shoe." She hopped to her feet and fixed her top. "Do you need a minute?"

"Ah...no. I'm good." He'd have to be. Adam pulled his trunks back on, wincing at the feeling of wet fabric against his skin.

"Cool. We better get back. I'm sure by this point, Aubry's decided that we've been murdered by an alligator or a serial killer or something to do with banjos."

How the hell could she be so bouncy when it felt like his entire world had been rocked to the core? Irritation rose at how keen she was to have everyone know exactly what they were just doing, even though he knew he had no right to it. This was what she'd wanted to begin with—scandal.

Well, oral sex in the woods with a party fifty feet away is pretty fucking scandalous.

Sheer pride kept him moving as he followed her back to the river. He searched for something to say. "Your friend is an odd one."

"We all like what we like. Aubry just likes her space and her computer and weird B horror movies and theories about how the world is going to end in a zombie apocalypse."

"Noted." That sounded weird as fuck to him, but who was he to judge? There were plenty of people that thought climbing on the back of a pissed-off bull was a study in insanity, and he'd done it more times than he could count. The truth was he never felt more alive than that second before the gate snapped open and the animal burst into motion.

Except for maybe when he was with Jules.

Damn it.

He held her tube so she could hop into it and then pushed them both out into the swimming hole. He wasn't sure what else there was to say. He'd just lost his mind and dragged her into the woods like a crazy person, and then she'd given him the single most devastating blowjob of his life. It wasn't even the technique—though that had been beyond reproach. It was the fact she seemed to be having such *fun* while she was doing it. Sex had been a lot of things for him in the past— intense, distracting, toxic—but never fun. He wasn't sure what to do with fun.

They paddled around the bend and there was the rest of their party, standing and bullshitting on the minuscule beach. Aubry stood away from the rest of them, her hand shielding the sun from her eyes as she searched—obviously for them. "Jules!"

"Shit," Jules muttered. They barely got within reach of the beach when she jumped out of the tube with a splash. "I'm fine. I didn't get eaten."

Quinn crossed over to them and gave Adam a long look.

"Are you sure about that?"

The choked sound Jules made had Aubry zeroing in on her. "Oh, we're going to have words, and soon."

"Great."

And then there came Grant, the pinched look around his mouth doing nothing to make Adam feel less like punching his face in. "Took you two long enough. We thought one of your tubes might have popped."

Jules's grin was bright enough to blind. "Nope. Nothing like that."

"I...see." Grant took her in with one long look and then turned the same expression on Adam. "You work fast, don't you?"

It didn't matter that Adam had been feeling kind of shitty about how things just played out. He wasn't about to have *this* asshole adding on the guilt. "None of your business."

"Oh, I think it is. I'm concerned for Jules."

The woman in question inserted herself between them, though Adam couldn't begin to say which of them she was planning on saving. "*Jules* is standing right here and can hear you both. Why don't we get moving? I'm working the second shift and I don't want to be late." She didn't give them a chance to argue, moving back to the tubes, Aubry on her heels. The redhead took Adam's tube, shooting him a sharp look over her shoulder. A look he fucking deserved.

Grant and his three chicks headed for the fire pit, leaving Adam and Quinn standing on the beach. Quinn crossed his arms over his chest. "Daniel's going to kill you."

"I don't know what you're talking about."

"You're not even bothering to lie well when you say that shit." He shook his head. "I'd get my story straight, and fast, because he's going to hear about this sooner rather than later. You know how this town works."

Yeah, he knew. Nothing stayed secret for long in Devil's

Falls—which had been exactly the point. But if Adam had half a brain in his head, he'd track Jules down tonight and explain nicely to her he couldn't do this anymore and that he was sorry for taking advantage of her in her obviously unstable emotional state.

That was the problem, though.

He wasn't sorry, and he didn't want to stop.

Chapter Ten

"I thought Adam was your *fake* boyfriend."

Jules had known this was coming the second she got out of Adam's truck. Frankly, she was surprised Aubry had waited until they were alone to pounce. She moved around the now-closed café, wiping down tables. Her cousin Jamie had already closed the till and taken off for some hot date, so it was just Jules and Aubry and the cats left. "We are."

"So you were having *fake* sex out in nature like horndog apes?"

She rolled her eyes. "We didn't have sex." Because *he* put on the brakes. She'd been so out of her mind with pleasure, she wasn't sure she would have been smart enough to call the whole thing off just because there wasn't a condom handy. And *that* was downright unforgivable. She wanted to be scandalous—not stupid. And having unprotected sex with a fake boyfriend, no matter how safe Adam made her feel, was stupid beyond belief.

"But you *wanted* to have sex."

Yes. She did. A lot. More than a lot. Jules scrubbed at a

coffee stain in the center of one table, pausing to nudge Ninja Kitteh out of the way when the striped cat came to snoop. "We're two consenting adults. I don't see how it matters."

"Totally not my point." Aubry double-checked the lock on the front door and headed for her table.

"Then, pray tell, what *is* your point?"

Her friend frowned. "I'm not judging—not really. That's not what we do. I just don't want to see you get hurt because your heart gets involved. That guy might be cool as hell—and he is—but he's spent a grand total of like a month in Devil's Falls in the last however many years. A guy like that doesn't have roots, and your roots are deeper than deep. You're not leaving this place and he's not staying."

"Don't project your relationship issues on me." As soon as the words were out of her mouth, she regretted them. "Oh my God, I'm a horrible friend for saying that. I'm sorry. I'm just so on edge with Grant and Adam and…there's no excuse. Forgive me?"

"Always." Aubry zipped the laptop case closed. "And you're right. I'm even more of a hot mess than you are when it comes to men. I'm just a Ford tough mama bear who's feeling protective. If he breaks your heart, I'm liable to set his truck on fire."

The scary part was that Jules wasn't exactly sure if her friend was joking or not. It was a step of crazy that Aubry would never take for herself—if she had, then her asshole ex would definitely have seen the results—but for Jules…yeah, she'd do that and worse. She walked over and hugged her friend. "I love you."

"I know. I love you, too. Just…be careful."

"I will. I promise." Even as she said the words, she knew they weren't the full truth. When it came to Adam, she was on a roller coaster and the safety brakes were gone. There was only one possible outcome, but she couldn't bring herself to care. It would be one heck of a ride before she crashed and burned.

"No, you won't, but that's okay." Aubry stepped back. "Do you have a hot date tonight, too, or can we *please* shoot some people? I have so much pent-up aggression after spending the afternoon trapped on that horrid body of water with the biggest asshat in town."

Jules laughed. "Grant's bad, but I don't know that he's *that* bad."

"One, yes, he is. Two, I wasn't talking about him."

Jules turned off the main lights in the café, leaving the one over the counter on. Even though she knew the cats didn't care, she didn't like leaving them in complete darkness. She checked the lock on the front door one last time and then followed Aubry through the kitchen and up the back stairs to their apartment. "Quinn isn't a bad guy. I think he's funny."

"Funny for a performing bear."

There was no arguing with her friend when she got like this. When it came to new people, Aubry was judge, jury, and executioner—nine times out of ten, she hated them on sight. Apparently she'd already passed judgment on Adam and Daniel's friend. To be fair, he seemed to really like getting a rise out of her. "If you say so."

"This is why we get along so well. You don't expect me to like people."

She unlocked the door at the top of the stairs and held it open. "You like me."

"You aren't *people*. You're *my* people. Totally different thing." Aubry dropped her laptop on the tiny dining room table and plopped down on the overstuffed couch taking up the majority of the equally tiny living room. "Let's do this."

"I don't suppose you want something like food before we start?"

"Food is for the weak."

Jules laughed. She should have known that would be the answer. "All the same, I'm going to order pizza. There's nothing in the fridge."

"I wish this place had more options for delivery. Little Johnny Jacob has started giving me judgmental looks when he brings me food."

"That's because you prefer to just order pizza instead of going down the street to one of our restaurants and interacting with real-life people."

Aubry turned on the Xbox and propped her feet on the table. "I believe we just covered this—people are not my favorite."

"Noted." Jules picked up her phone and froze when there was a knock on her door. "Okay, I know Johnny Jacob is good, but no one is *that* good." She walked over and opened the door and then stared. "What are you doing here?"

Adam stood on the top stair, looking all sorts of delicious with his worn jeans and black T-shirt. He held up hands laden with beer and a pizza box sending out the most amazing smells. "I brought pizza and beer."

"Let him in," Aubry yelled from behind her. "I'm liable to waste away from starvation if I don't eat soon. They'll find me on the couch, and there will be whispers of, 'If only Jules had let her fake boyfriend inside in time. Such a tragedy.'"

"I thought you said food was for the weak." She stepped back, holding the door open for Adam. "You're an awful drama queen—and inconsistent to boot."

"Noted," Aubry sang a second before the sound of video game gunshots filled the room.

Jules led Adam over to the small kitchen and grabbed three of the bright plastic plates that made her mother cringe every time she saw them. She opened the pizza box and put two slices on each plate while Adam popped the tops off three beers. They deposited the food and beer in front of Aubry, but she shook her head. "You two need to talk. Git."

"Did you just say 'git'?" There went Adam's eyebrow.

"Don't you, like, ride bulls or something? You're a cowboy. I'm speaking your language." She tore her gaze away from the screen for half a second. "Seriously, though—what kind of death wish do you have that you'd climb onto the back of a pissed-off bull? Did your daddy not tell you he loves you enough?"

Jules saw the tightening in Adam's jaw and the way his shoulders braced ever so slightly. She shifted her grip on the plates and touched his arm. "Let's go into my room." When he turned toward her door, she shot a glare at Aubry and hissed, "Stop being rude." Jules didn't give her friend time to respond before she nudged Adam fully into her room and shut the door.

Looking around, she realized this was the dumbest plan ever. They had to step over her dirty clothes pile to get to the bed, which was covered in her *clean* clothes pile. *Probably should have found time to fold laundry in the last week.* She couldn't let him sit there while she scrambled to put away her clothes and unmentionables. It didn't matter if he'd had his mouth on the same parts of her that those unmentionables covered. It was just *weird*.

She skirted the edge of the bed and moved to the window. "Sorry about the mess."

"It's fine." But he was looking at everything like he was committing it to memory. With her luck, that was exactly what he was doing. She set the plates down long enough to muscle open the window. *That* got Adam's attention. "What are you doing?"

"Come on." She slipped out the window and reached back in to grab the plates. A few seconds later, Adam joined her on the roof. "I like to come out here and think sometimes."

He peered over the edge to where they could see the

majority of the main street. "And spy on the poor people of Devil's Falls. No wonder there's so much gossip."

She started to argue but then laughed. "Maybe a little spying. People stumble out from the bar"—that didn't actually have a name beyond "the bar"—"and they forget that sound travels." Jules took a sip of her beer. "Plus, no one ever sees me up here."

"Fair enough." He went after his pizza with the single-minded focus of someone who didn't know when their next meal would be—or who wanted to avoid conversation.

The problem was that avoiding conversations wasn't something Jules was particularly good at. She would rather burst through the awkwardness like the Kool-Aid Man came through the wall—all at once, just to get it over with. It wasn't subtle, but subtlety wasn't really in her skill set. "So, I don't know what to think of what happened earlier."

He chewed his bite and swallowed, not looking at her. "You mean when you came against my mouth and then sucked me off."

Her body flushed hot. *Guess he's not great at being subtle, either.* "Yeah, that." He didn't immediately jump in with something reassuring, so she just kept talking. "It was good. It was really, really good. I just, ah—"

"I'm not staying."

The words came out so harshly she had to take a moment to fight back her instinctive response. Finally, she said, "I never asked you to."

"Right." He set the plate down and stretched out his legs. "So, now that we've gotten that out of the way—"

Is he serious? "Adam, we have to talk about this. I mean, obviously we're not dating for real, and I don't exactly go hook up with almost strangers on the fly under normal circumstances. I just…" God, she didn't even know what she was trying to say.

"Sugar, breathe." He took her hand, the contact steadying her. "It's okay. We don't have to go there. I lost control. I'll make sure it doesn't happen again."

That was *not* what she wanted. Jules bit her lip, searching his face. In the fading light of the day, his eyes were too dark as he stared at her mouth. He wanted her. He wouldn't have lost control in the first place if he didn't. So why was he trying to give her an out?

For such a supposed bad boy, he's sure got a lot of honor.

The realization struck a chord in her chest. She finished off her beer and set it carefully aside. "I don't want you to have control." Before he could do anything but frown at her, she crawled over and straddled him. "Look, I know this isn't real. I obviously have no experience in this sort of thing or I wouldn't need to scandalize the town in the first place." She took his hands and set them on her hips. "Why don't we just enjoy ourselves while you're helping me out?"

His lips twitched, but his grip tightened on her hips a little. "Sugar, we don't have to do this. We can keep the gossip mill churning without taking things beyond where we went earlier."

Yeah, there really is *an honorable man in there.* "I know, but I want to." She could feel him growing hard between her thighs, and she settled against him with a little sigh. Jules leaned forward until her breasts were pressed against his chest. She felt a little silly trying to proposition him, but he wasn't tossing her on her butt, so she must not be doing too badly. She held her breath and kissed the spot on his neck right below his jaw. "Adam, I would very much like to have sex with you."

Chapter Eleven

Adam could hardly believe this shit was happening. If he was a better man, he'd set her aside and explain why this would only end in tears for her. Jules wasn't the type of woman to be able to get to a certain level of physical intimacy without her heart becoming involved. He liked her. He didn't want to hurt her.

But he wasn't a better man.

She's a grown-ass woman. She knows her own mind.

It was an excuse and a weak one at that. He didn't care. For all his words, he didn't want to stop this any more than she did. But he still held back. He wrapped his fist in her hair, using the leverage to guide her back so she had to meet his gaze. "You're sure about this?"

"I wouldn't say it if I wasn't."

He didn't quite believe her, but he allowed himself to be persuaded. "Come here, sugar." He wrapped an arm around her waist and scooted them away from the edge of the roof until his back hit the side of the house. From here, no one on the street below could see them.

Scandal be damned, I'm not about giving them a peep show.

He coasted his hands up her sides, lifting her shirt as he did. He checked her expression when he hit the same level as her breasts, but there was nothing but eagerness there. So he pulled her shirt over her head and dropped it next to them.

She gave a little cry when he took off her bra, at once eager and needy, and that nearly undid him on the spot. He knew this wasn't supposed to be real. Except it sure as hell *felt* real when he helped her wiggle out of her jeans and resume her position straddling him.

It felt all too real. He ran his hand down the center of her body, between her breasts, over her stomach, to cup her pussy. Adam groaned when he found her hot and wet. "You drive me to distraction."

"Sorry."

"Don't be." This being a distraction was supposed to be the point. He pumped first one finger and then two into her. "I enjoy the hell out of it. Wear a dress next time we go out, sugar, and I'll do this to you while I drive us around."

Her eyes had drifted half shut, her hands gripping his shoulders. "I think that qualifies as distracted driving."

"Nah, I'll take care of you." He shifted his movements, exploring until he found the exact motion that made her body jerk taut. "Like that."

"Oh God." Her hips rolled, trying to take him deeper, but he'd found the sweet spot and he wasn't about to let go of her until he was ready. "I've been thinking about licking that sweet little pussy of yours against that tree."

"Adam!"

He grinned, amazed that she could sound so shocked while obviously enjoying their current circumstances. "Lesson two in dirty talking—learn to say 'pussy' and 'cock.'"

"C-c—" She made a face. "Cock. See! I can say it."

Hearing the word on her lips was like she'd reached down and squeezed that part of him. He kept finger fucking her, fighting to get the words out through clenched teeth. "Unzip me, sugar. I want to feel you stroking me when you say it again."

Her eyes went wide, but she obeyed, carefully unzipping his jeans and sliding them down far enough to free him. Her first stroke was almost tentative, but he kept her too distracted with what he was doing between her legs to be self-conscious. "Say it again."

"Cock." This time there was no hesitation or stuttering.

"Mmm. And whose cock are you stroking right now?"

"Y-yours."

He pulled her closer, the move dislodging both their hands, and guided his cock between her legs, the position too tight for him to enter her. He lined them up so he rubbed against her clit and grabbed a hold of her hips, rocking her against him.

Watching the pleasure on her face was almost reward enough. Almost. "Tell me what you want, sugar. Explicitly."

She bit her lip. "I want you—your cock—inside me."

He had to hold still for a second to fight back the need to give her exactly that right that second. "And how do you want it?"

"I...don't know."

It struck him that it might be the fucking truth. How in God's name had a hot little thing like Jules Rodriguez made it to twenty-six without knowing what she liked? He kept moving her against him, driving them both crazy. "You have one of those buzzy toys?"

It was hard to tell in the shadows, but she looked like she might be blushing furiously. "I have several."

At least she wasn't shy about meeting her needs while solo. He kissed her neck. "And how do you like using them?"

"I…" Her breath hitched. "God, that feels good."

"I'm not going to stop. Answer the question."

She shivered. "I tease myself. Until I can barely stand it. Then I…"

He gently bit her earlobe. "Keep going."

"Then I stroke myself as hard as I can."

Adam groaned. He could perfectly picture her like that, naked in her bed alone, stroking herself with some toy until she came apart. "I'm going to make it good for you, sugar."

"Then *hurry*."

He dug into his pocket for the condom he'd thought he was an idiot for bringing tonight. It was a study in frustration to let her go long enough to rip open the wrapper and roll it on, but he managed.

She started to sink onto him, but he stopped her. "Last chance."

"And for the last time, I want this. I want *you*."

He knew she only meant it in this moment, but it still struck a chord deep inside him. When had he last felt wanted by a woman—him as a man, not as a conduit of pleasure? Had he ever? He let go of her, and she sank onto his cock, inch by inch, until they were sealed as closely as two people could be. "Fuck, sugar, you feel so good. Better than I could have dreamed."

"Yes." She lifted up and slammed back onto him, but their position made it difficult to get a good momentum going.

He rolled them, laying her down on her clothes, and thrust into her. "You want it hard?"

"*Yes.*" The word was barely more than a moan on her lips. "Like that."

He fucked her with everything he had in him, slamming into her until he had to muffle her cries with his hand. She consumed him, her summer scent wrapping around him, her muffled cries in his ear, the taste of her on his tongue. He couldn't get enough, couldn't stop, couldn't slow down. He needed her orgasm more than he needed his next breath.

"Adam, oh my God, Adam, don't stop." Her nails dug into his ass, urging him on. As if he was in any danger of stopping.

"I won't, sugar." He kissed her again, holding her as tightly as he could, until her entire body went tight and she came, her pussy milking him and dragging him over the edge. Desire consumed him, leaving nothing but ashes in its wake.

• • •

Jules was pretty sure she heard baby angels singing and that the heavens opened up to shine on her.

Or maybe that had just been a truly outstanding orgasm.

She lifted her head and looked at Adam, who seemed just as floored as she felt. Maybe that was wishful thinking on her part, but he kissed her before she could overthink things too much. "How are you doing?"

"Well and truly satisfied."

His grin made things low in her stomach clench, which made his jaw go tight, which made her hot all over again. Adam stroked a hand up her side, idly cupping her breast and circling her nipple. "You have anywhere to be in the next hour?"

Hour? She shifted. The fact they were having this conversation while he was still inside her wasn't in her realm of social niceties. "Uh, no?"

"Perfect." He kissed her again, his tongue sliding along hers. "Because I'm nowhere near done with you."

Sweet baby Jesus. She just stared as he got to his knees and pulled his pants back up. "You're not?"

"Sugar, I know it might be shocking, but I'd like to have sex with you while we're both naked and have full range of motion." His grin made her toes curl. "Not that I'm even remotely complaining about how things just went down."

She should have known that letting go of her previous expectations was important when it came to this man, but obviously she hadn't managed it, because he kept surprising her. "Okay." She licked her lips and peered down at the street below them. "Do you think someone heard us?"

"Sugar, focus." He pulled her to her feet, and she didn't miss the fact that he stood between her and the edge of the roof, blocking the sight of anyone who bothered to look up. She almost pointed out that someone catching a glimpse of her up here with him in an obvious state of undress would surely get tongues wagging, but the look on his face stopped her.

Stop overthinking. Just enjoy this. You got an orgasm for the record books.

And he wants an hour to do it again.

She stifled a giggle and ducked back into her room, pausing long enough to make sure she could still hear the gunshot sounds and music from Aubry's game. Satisfied that her friend wasn't going to come barging in to save her or something, she turned to face Adam. "You want me focused? I'm focused."

"Perfect." He scooped her up and dropped her on the bed, scattering her laundry and surprising a laugh out of her.

She propped herself up on her elbows and watched him strip. His eyebrows rose. "When you look at me like that, I feel like a piece of meat."

"Not just any meat—grade-A prime rib."

If anything, his eyebrows rose higher. "You're something else."

"Something awesome." It had to be the orgasm going to her head, because she felt positively punch-drunk. "Now get over here and lay one on me."

He crawled onto the bed, his muscles flexing beneath

golden skin. "Oh, sugar, I'm about to lay something on you all right."

She barely waited for him to kiss her before she pushed on his shoulders. "Wait, wait, wait. You promised I'd get to be on top. It's most definitely my turn now."

"I'm not going to argue with that." He flopped onto his back, pulling her with him so that she sprawled over his chest. Adam's eyebrow cocked up, a grin pulling at the edges of his lips. "Well, you have me at your mercy. What are you going to do with me?"

Everything. With all his skin laid out for her enjoyment, she didn't know where to start. She sat up so she could see more of him and trailed her hands down his chest, watching the way his muscles jumped beneath her touch. He had the body of a man who *worked*, his muscles clearly defined without being over-the-top. "I'm going to have some fun." More fun than should be legal.

Adam's gaze traveled over her breasts, making her nipples pebble and her skin tingle. "You have a very limited time before I toss you down and have my way with you."

"I thought I was in charge here."

He rested his hands on her sides, his thumb tracing her hipbones. "You're enough to tempt a saint to sin, sugar. And I'm nowhere near a saint." He stroked up her sides to cup her breasts. "Though I like the view too much to stop—you're right on that note. The sight of you sliding up and down my cock… Yeah, I'm willing to take a backseat for that."

Funny, but it didn't feel like he was in the backseat while coaxing little shivers from her body by kneading her breasts. Jules arched her back, pressing herself more fully into his palms. "Don't stop."

"I won't." But he paused. "I don't suppose you have condoms in this place?"

Her cheeks heated, but she wasted no time scrambling for

the top drawer of her nightstand. When she got there, though, she paused. For all her optimism of getting laid sometime this decade, she hadn't even bothered to take the cellophane off the box. Jules shot Adam a look, but there was no way she could unwrap it without him hearing and/or seeing.

But the alternative was to not have sex with Adam again, so…

Jules decided right then and there that she could afford a little dose of humiliation with *that* carrot dangling in front of her.

She ripped into the wrapper, tearing it off like a kid with a Christmas present. "I am only 75 percent prepared. Don't judge me. They didn't cover this in Girl Scouts."

His laugh rolled through the room, foreplay all on its own. "Never a dull moment."

"Wouldn't dream of it." She finally freed the box and yanked out a condom. Or, rather, she yanked out a string of a dozen condoms. Jules held it up, feeling sheepish. "How are we looking for an hour's worth of time?"

Just like that, the amusement was gone from Adam's face, replaced by desire. "Why don't you get that sweet ass of yours over here and find out?"

Lord, but she was more than happy to do exactly that.

Chapter Twelve

"You're going out with the Rodriguez girl again, aren't you?"

Adam paused in the middle of shoving a bottle of wine into a backpack. There was absolutely no reason to feel guilty. Jules knew this was temporary. Hell, if anyone should feel hurt, it was him, because it seemed like every time he turned around, she was going on about making a scene and creating a scandal. *That* was her focus, not falling head over heels for him. But none of that stopped the slow turn of his stomach when he straightened to face his mama. "Yeah."

She searched his face, her brown eyes somehow seeming faded, like a part of her had already given up. "Good."

He blinked. "What?"

"You've got two ears in your head, son. You heard me just fine." She turned around and wobbled to the recliner. "Jules is a good girl."

He followed, still half sure he'd heard her wrong. "Which is exactly the reason you told me to stay the hell away from her before this point."

"Maybe things have changed."

"Nothing's changed." He helped her sit down. There had been another doctor's appointment this morning, and, like all the others, she wouldn't let him come with her. He tried really hard not to resent his mama's decision, but it was a chicken bone stuck in his throat. It wasn't like he didn't know exactly how bad things were. Hearing it from the doctor firsthand wouldn't change anything.

Except maybe it would. Maybe it would make everything a whole hell of a lot more real. Maybe I'd lose my shit.

Or maybe there'd be some avenue to pursue that my mama refuses to try.

He looked at the backpack he'd been stuffing with things for his date with Jules, suddenly feeling like the lowest piece of shit in existence. "I don't have to go."

"Adam—"

"You're right. I shouldn't. I'll go get us some dinner and we'll watch that chick flick you've been tittering about with Lenora—the one with that guy who writes letters to his girlfriend while he's away at war." It sounded boring as hell, but it wasn't about what he wanted.

Her hand on his arm stopped him, her grip surprisingly strong. "No."

"But, Mama—"

"*No.*" She shook her head. "I love you, my boy, but you can't stop living just because I'm sick. You're here for me and that's all that matters. Go take your girl out, show her a good time, get into a little trouble. *Live.*"

He looked down at her, recognizing the stubborn set of her mouth. It was the same one he saw in the mirror when he'd made a decision he wouldn't be swayed from. She wanted him out of the house tonight and going to spend time with Jules. He might not get her reasons, but he wasn't going to be able to change her mind. "If you're sure."

"I am. Lenora is coming over. We want to cuddle and

critique the movie alone." Her expression softened into a small smile. "It would be a dreadfully boring night for you."

"Time spent with you is anything but boring."

Her eyes shone a little. "Baby, you're the best son a woman could ask for."

"Yeah, well, I had the best mama a boy could dream of." And if he didn't get the fuck out of here, the barbed ball of emotion in his chest might actually break free. He'd done a damn good job of keeping it locked down since he found out she was sick, and he had no intention of letting it out anytime soon. He covered her hand with his and squeezed. "You call me if you need anything."

"I will."

There was nothing left to do but leave. Adam zipped up the backpack and walked out the front door without looking back. He'd learned a long time ago that a final glance over his shoulder was a great way to have regrets dogging his heels every step of the way.

• • •

Jules was finishing up her shift when Adam pulled up to the curb. There was something really sexy about that man in an obviously well-loved truck that had seen him through the years. Had it been the only thing he'd kept with him all that time? Her heart gave a funny lurch at the thought, and she turned back to lock the front door to cover the reaction.

It's just because we had sex. I've always been awful at keeping emotions out of it…probably because I never thought to try.

"Looks like your boyfriend is here!" Jamie sang from her place by the register. She grinned from ear to ear when Jules shushed her. "What? This is the most exciting thing to happen to you in your entire life. I know everyone loves Grant, but you traded up, girl!"

She shushed her cousin again, trying to ignore the buoyancy Jamie's words brought and turned back to find Adam within reachable distance. Jules tugged at the bottom of her sundress, not sure what to do with her hands. Was she supposed to kiss him? Wave? A freaking handshake?

Adam took the decision away from her, hooking the small of her back and pulling her against him. "Hey."

"Hey." She frowned. "Are you okay? You look like you haven't been sleeping." She'd been having a hell of a time getting shut-eye, but that was all self-induced. Every time she closed her eyes, she was assaulted with memories of their time together. Her trusty friend B.O.B. had been getting a solid workout as a result.

But Adam didn't look like he'd spent far too much time wanking it. He looked…haunted.

His mouth tightened. "I thought we covered the fact that I hate that question."

They had. But a silly part of her thought that maybe things would have changed because of last night. She forced a smile. "My mistake." It hurt, though. It didn't matter that she had no right to the emotion—it still burrowed deep, twining through her and squeezing hard enough that she could barely draw a breath for one eternal second. "So what's on the agenda tonight?"

He held up a backpack. "Moonlight picnic."

Jules blinked. "That sounds…" Romantic. Which it most certainly couldn't be, because he'd been very clear about what this thing was. The hurt still lingering from him shutting her down had her mouth getting away from her, "Explain to me how that's going to get Grant off my back?"

"Sugar, it's going to be a good time."

That wasn't an answer. And she had no doubt it *would* be a good time—too good a time. They'd had sex a grand total of twenty-four hours ago, and she was already having trouble keeping her emotions inside that cute little boundary fence she'd constructed. No, the very last thing Jules needed was a romantic picnic with Adam. She straightened her shoulders and started down the street. "Okay, then." She headed to the door. "Call me if you need anything, Jamie."

"I won't!"

She pushed out into the early summer heat, driven by the messy emotions turning her insides into a maze of confusion.

"Where are you going?"

She didn't know, but her gaze landed on the bar and inspiration struck. "I'm going to go take some shots."

"What?" He caught up with her, matching her pace. "What's gotten into you?"

Just that you're sending mixed messages like whoa, and I can't deal with it. I also can't tell *you that you're sending mixed messages, because you flat-out told me that this couldn't be anything, and I'm an idiot for looking too much into a theoretical moonlit picnic because it's all about the plan.*

But she couldn't say that aloud. It sounded crazy in her head, and giving it voice would just confirm that she was a basket case. "I'm giving people something to talk about. If you want to go on a romantic picnic afterward, fine." She crossed the street and pushed through the front door.

Jules didn't spend much time in the bar because Aubry was kind of a shut-in and preferred to drink in her comfort zone. Plus…why would she walk down the street and pay double for alcohol she could just buy at the store? Especially when the bar's wine selection left something to be desired.

She eyed the scattering of people. There were Kelli and Kelly over by the jukebox, dancing all slow and sexy with each other. *Maybe I was wrong and they* like *like each other.* But then they shifted and Jules nearly cursed. Grant. Because *of course* Grant would be there. As she was trying to figure out the best course of action, he lifted his head and met her gaze.

Crap. There was nothing for it. If she turned around and bolted, he'd know he was the reason. She felt Adam's presence at her back, as comforting as it was aggravating. *When in doubt, rush ahead as quickly as possible.* Good, sound advice that had gotten her into more awkward situations than she cared to count.

She looked around the room a second time, searching for salvation. A group of old-timers huddled around the bar, and she recognized her uncle Rodger, Daniel's dad. *Perfect.* "Uncle Rodger!" Jules sailed over and gave him a hug. He was a giant bear of a man who, with his long hair, craggy face, and beard, would look at home in some illicit motorcycle club. And he made the best cupcakes this side of the Mississippi. "What are you doing here?"

"Poker night." He lifted her off her feet and squeezed. "You've lost weight, Julie Q."

"Guess you better make me a dozen of those red velvet cupcakes. Better yet, make it two dozen."

He gave a great laugh. "I'll do that." The smile fell away from his face as he set her down and looked over her shoulder. "I heard a rumor you were dating that Meyer boy, but I didn't believe it. Tell your uncle Rodger it isn't so."

The only way they could get Grant to believe it was to get the entire town to believe it. Jules didn't like lying to her family, but it was only a tiny, white lie. "What can I say? He's swept me off my feet."

"I bet." One of the men behind Rodger snickered, but the sound died quickly when her uncle leveled a glare over his shoulder.

He sighed. "I suppose you're too old to have me threatening him with my shotgun? Your daddy and I were dying to do that song and dance back when you were in high school, but that Thomas boy didn't seem like that much of a threat." His brows slanted down over his eyes. "But then he went and broke your heart."

Jules had never wanted lightning to strike her on the spot so badly as she did in that moment. "That's so great that you're going to trot out my past humiliations for everyone's amusement, but that's ancient history—and no, you don't get to play big badass uncle and try to scare Adam away. I like him." *Possibly too much.*

"That's what I'm afraid of. You know it's my job to look out for you while your parents are off living the big-city life."

"They only moved six hours away, and we see them once a month."

"Too far, if you ask me."

If they'd asked her, it was, too, but it hadn't been her decision. She missed her parents like whoa, but her mom always entertained her with stories about new restaurants they were trying and how she'd talked her dad into taking a salsa class, and Jules couldn't help but be happy for them. They were happy.

Adam's arm settled around her waist, and her entire body sparked to life. God, she was in so much trouble. This close, she got a whiff of his spicy cologne, and it smelled like something a cowboy in a commercial would wear—manly and rough and…what the heck was she thinking?

Jules started to move away, but he tightened his hold on her. "Rodger."

"Adam." Her uncle eyed the arm around her waist, almost like he was considering whether to make an issue of it or not. Apparently he decided Jules was a grown woman and could make her own decisions—or, more likely, he was going to go straight to the nearest phone to tattle on her to her parents. "Y'all have a good night."

"We will." She grinned so hard that her cheeks hurt. "And

on that note…shots!"

"Sugar—"

She ignored Adam and slipped out of his hold. The bartender winked at her. "Hey, darlin'. I haven't seen much of you these days."

It took Jules a whole second to place him. "Stuart! I thought you up and moved to San Antonio."

"I did." He grinned, his teeth bright against his dark skin. "I went, I saw, now I'm back. Devil's Falls is a siren call that I couldn't ignore." He gave her a long, slow look. "You're looking good."

"She's also looking taken."

Jules rolled her eyes. "Stuart, this is Adam. We're dating." *Sort of.* "Adam, this is Stuart. We went to high school together."

"Holy shit. I heard you were taking a walk on the wild side, but seeing is believing." He leaned across the bar and lowered his voice until she could barely hear him. "I have to say, I thought for sure you were going to marry Grant and pop out a couple kids."

Yeah, she knew. That's what everyone had thought after graduation, and probably again now that he was back in town.

Not. Interested.

This was exactly why she'd come up with this insane plan to begin with. The only problem was that she had a feeling proving them all wrong was going to come back to bite her in her butt, because Adam was a wildfire that would burn her up if she wasn't careful.

And a tiny part of her wanted to douse herself in gasoline and welcome the flames.

Chapter Thirteen

Adam wasn't sure when the night had taken a turn for the what-the-fuck, but Jules seemed determined to throw herself into getting shit-housed drunk to be *scandalous*. She was three shots down and weaving on her feet. He recognized that look in her eye, though. There would be no backing down, and if he tried to derail her, it would backfire.

Whoever put it into the woman's head that she was on the shelf was a goddamn fool.

"How about—"

"You're right. Stuart, another purple nurple!"

Stuart shot him a wide-eyed look but started pouring Jules another of the sickeningly sweet shots. Adam wasn't sure why she couldn't just shoot whiskey. It was a classic. He leaned against the bar. It was time to distract her before he had to carry her out of here over his shoulder. "So you're planning on showing Grant up by, what, getting blackout drunk and passing out facedown in a pile of your own puke?"

"Ew, gross. No." She made a face and then had to catch herself on the bar when she swayed too much to one side.

"Don't be silly. I'm stunning him with my amazing drinking abilities."

"Amazing is one way to put it." At least her uncle had left ten minutes ago. The man had been staring at him intently enough that Adam was half sure he'd walk out the door and find Rodger and his friends waiting for him. "Why don't we head back to your place?"

She shook her head. Well, she shook her entire body. "Not yet. I want to play darts. Or maybe start a bar fight. That's a thing people do in bars, isn't it?" She frowned. "I don't get out much, and Aubry is the one who starts fights, so I never get to drink too much and let go. Let's let go tonight!"

A fight was not on the books, and letting her drunk ass anywhere near pointy objects was the worst idea he'd ever heard. Adam looked around the bar, searching for inspiration. He'd never realized how many potential weapons there were just sitting around until he had a drunk good girl wanting to get into some trouble. "Bar fights are overrated."

"*God.*" She grabbed the shot Stuart set on the bar and downed it before Adam could blink. "Of course you've been in a bar fight. I bet you've been in a ton."

More than he cared to remember, all for reasons he *couldn't* remember. He didn't drink much these days, but in his early twenties, he'd been angry and felt like he had something to prove. Trouble had been his middle name, and he'd gone looking for it every chance he had.

Hell, that was why he'd started riding bulls to begin with. That moment before the gates slammed open, he wasn't thinking about how tight his skin got when he stayed in one place too long or the sad look in his mama's eyes when she realized he was itching to leave Devil's Falls again. There was just Adam and the bull and the next few seconds of freedom and adrenaline.

When had his life gotten so empty?

He worked to keep the smile on his face. "It's overrated."

"I wouldn't know." Her expression was so woeful, he almost laughed. She instantly brightened. "I love this song!"

He hadn't even been aware of the song changing, and then she was off, shooting around him and veering to the dance floor where she started... He stared. Only someone being really, *really* nice would call that dancing. She looked like a marionette whose strings were cut, all jarring motions and jerking limbs.

It might have been the cutest thing he'd ever seen. Awkward. Horribly awkward. But cute.

Adam sighed. "I need a beer."

Almost instantly, one appeared at his elbow. Stuart didn't immediately move away. "She's a good girl."

"So I keep hearing." Along with the part no one but his mama seemed to be able to say. He *wasn't* good. Oh, he wasn't bad. But he wasn't anywhere near Jules's level. She practically shone with goodness. Hell, she owned a business whose sole purpose was to make people happy—and she'd managed to rescue half a dozen cats in the process. She was so sweet, it should make his teeth ache.

But then he thought about her sunny smile that only seemed to appear when he was inside her.

Adam's body kicked into high gear, and it was everything he could do to keep his reaction from physically manifesting. He turned away from the bar, beer in hand, to find Grant on the edge of the dance floor. Whatever the man said had Jules's back going straight and her shoulders going back in a stance he recognized. *Shit.*

He strode across the bar, arriving at her side in time to hear Grant say, "Jesus, Jules, it was a joke. Obviously I wasn't being serious."

There were tears shining in her eyes, and the sight of them snapped something inside Adam. He moved between her and her ex. "You know what, I'm getting really tired of your brand of shit."

Grant took a step back before he seemed to catch himself. "It's not my fault Jules is drunk and took it wrong."

"You offered to *let* me give you a BJ in the bathroom!"

Just like that, any good intentions Adam had went up in smoke—and there hadn't been many to begin with. "You think you're a big-time operator because you played ball, then went off to a fancy school and got yourself a law degree. Guess what? You're still back in Devil's Falls, the same as everyone in this bar. You're no better than anyone else. In fact, you're a whole hell of a lot worse."

"And what have *you* done? Thirty-three and a washed-up bull rider." Grant sneered. "I'm sure there's an opening at the Gas 'N' Go for the night shift."

"Oh, no, you didn't!"

Adam made a grab for Jules, but she slipped through his hands like water. And then she was in Grant's face, poking him in the chest. "Damn you to hell and back, Grant Thomas. I know for a fact your mama raised you not to talk to your betters like that."

He shook his head. "If you're not going to put that mouth to good use, then go home, Jules. You're making a spectacle of yourself." And then he was gone, walking out of the bar like he hadn't a care in the world.

Adam started after him but stopped, his need to make sure Jules didn't take a nosedive superseding his desire to beat that jackass's face in. He turned to find her pointing at the two blondes seated at the table Grant had occupied before all this got started. "You can't seriously think that's sexy."

The one on the right shrugged. "He's hot."

"He's an idiot." The other one laughed. "But he buys us all the alcohol we can drink."

"Good lord, that's a low bar to set." Jules threw up her

hands. "I don't even know why I bother."

The first one cocked her head to the side. "Because you're nice?"

"I need another shot."

Adam snagged her around the waist. "Hold your horses, sugar. You drink any more tonight and you're going to have to scrape yourself off the floor in the morning."

"Don't care."

"You might not right now, but you will when you wake up hugging a toilet." He hauled her to the bar and dug out the cash to pay for their tab. "We're getting out of here." Hopefully the fresh air would sober her up a little.

They hit the street, and he kept his arm around her in case the world decided to start spinning on her. Jules marched ahead, though, practically dragging him behind her, keeping up an ongoing rant about Grant. "I can't believe him. It's like he came back into town solely to rain on my parade. I *like* my life. I'm happy. I have a plan that I'm totally on track with. Why does he have to show up and make me feel like I'm failing?"

"Why do you care so much?" That's the thing that really bugged him. The town was one thing, but she *really* cared what Grant thought of her. The guy made a few dickhead comments and here she was, creating a fake relationship and doing all sorts of crazy shit to prove him wrong.

Was she holding a flame for the guy?

Adam's stomach turned at the thought. People didn't jump through the sheer number of hoops that Jules had unless there were lingering feelings. There was no damn good reason for the knowledge to burn him up inside, but he felt like he'd swallowed a dozen hot coals.

While he was aggravated as all get-out, she stopped and leaned back against his chest. "I don't want to go home."

He couldn't take her back to his mom's house, and he

didn't have a place of his own. He walked them to his truck and opened the driver's side door to double-check under the seat. Sure enough, there were two thick blankets under there. Most of the time, he forked over the money for a hotel room, but there were the nights when he chose the solitude of his truck over dealing with that bullshit. "You want to go for a ride?"

"A ride, huh?" She turned in his arms and waggled her eyebrows at him. Or she tried to.

Adam shook his head and lifted her into the truck. "Not like that, sugar. You're drunk as a skunk."

"Which means it's the perfect time for some nooky."

Maybe under different circumstances. But she was too drunk for a yes to really be a yes, and, fake girlfriend or not, he wasn't the kind of man who was into that sort of thing. Tonight she didn't need sex. She needed someone to take care of her. "Scoot over." He followed her up into the cab and shut the door.

Five minutes later, they left the town limits of Devil's Falls in the rearview mirror. He took them out to one of the spots that had been his favorite as a teenager. He and his friends had spent more nights than he could count out on the edge of this field, drinking and bullshitting and passing out in the beds of their trucks. He shut off the engine and stared at the stars while the engine ticked. "He's not worth it."

"Hmm?" She scooted over and burrowed under his arm to lean against his side.

"Grant. He's not worth it. You're so far out of his league, it's not even funny." *Out of both our leagues.*

A soft snore was his only response. Despite everything, he smiled. She really was something else. He'd never put much thought into the kind of woman he'd eventually settle down with—or into settling down in general. But he could almost picture it with Jules. Life would never be boring, that was for damn sure.

As if on cue, the restlessness in his blood kicked up a notch, like an itch he could never quite scratch, reminding him that he'd been in the same place for two weeks, longer than he'd spent in one town in twelve years. If his mom…

No, it's time to face the truth. It's not an if. It's a when. If the cancer doesn't take her, old age will at some point.

When his mom died…

Adam pulled Jules more tightly against him and rested his chin on the top of her head. He could barely stand to think the thought. How the hell would he be able to spend time in Devil's Falls when every time he turned around, he'd be assaulted with memories of her and have to experience the loss all over again? It had been unbearable after John died. With his mom it would be so much worse.

Even if she lived to the ripe old age of a hundred, the open road was too tempting a siren call for him to ignore for long. He needed the horizon stretching out before him, the thrill of the next bull ride promising an adrenaline rush like no other.

The closest he'd come to it outside the rodeo was the woman in his arms, and hell if that didn't make him a dick for using her to quell his thrill-seeking nature. It couldn't last, though. Nothing had kept him in one place for long before, and he didn't imagine anything would in the future.

No, he wasn't staying. He couldn't.

Chapter Fourteen

Jules woke up wonderfully warm…and certain that some small animal had crawled into her mouth and died. She shifted, not quite willing to leave the safe circle of Adam's arms — because she'd know that spicy scent anywhere.

"Morning."

She looked up, finding him far too close to risk opening her mouth. There was no help for it. She slithered out of his hold and to the other side of the bench seat. Eyeing the distance between them, she decided caution was the better part of valor and held her hand in front of her mouth. "Morning."

His eyebrows crept up. "What are you doing?"

Being an idiot, apparently. Considering what she remembered of the night before, he shouldn't be surprised. "Morning breath."

If anything, he looked even more amused. "Here." He opened the glove compartment and pulled out a bottle of water, a tiny toothbrush, and a travel-size tube of toothpaste.

She was so shocked, she dropped her hand. "You carry around a toothbrush setup in your truck?"

"As you said…morning breath. It's always good to have a backup ready if I'm not in a hotel room for whatever reason." He passed them over and waited while she considered. "If you're one of those people who are weird about toothbrushes—"

"No, it's fine." Considering where both their mouths had been on each other in the last week, sharing a toothbrush shouldn't be a big deal. It just felt kind of…domestic. Intimate.

Or maybe she was so hungover, she was thinking crazy thoughts.

Jules climbed out of the truck and went to work, brushing away until her mouth felt minty clean and there wasn't a trace of morning breath left. Then she waited while Adam did the same. It gave her the opportunity to really remember how much of a hot mess she'd been the night before. Regret soured her stomach—or maybe that was the purple nurples. "I think I'm dying."

He spit. "Nah, you're just feeling the effects of too much alcohol in too little time." He gave her some serious side eye. "Not going to lie—you were in rare form last night."

"Sorry." She should have just gone with the moonlight picnic. There was probably good food involved, and there *definitely* had to have been sex on the books. Instead she'd gotten drunk and made a fool of herself in front of half the town. *Talk about making a scene. I'm surprised I haven't already gotten a call from Jamie—or worse, Mom.* She didn't even want to look at her phone in case she was wrong.

Wait. Jules patted her pockets. Oh, crap. Her *phone*. She didn't have it. Aubry must have been going crazy imagining all the ways Jules might have been killed when she didn't come home. Hopefully she'd assume she spent the night with Adam.

She was *definitely* going to hear about this when she got back to the apartment.

He held the door open for her. "Happens to the best of

us."

Maybe. But it never happened with her—mostly because even if she got particularly drunk, her bed was only a handful of steps away. *I'm never drinking in public again.* Her stomach made a truly embarrassing sound and she glared at it. "Shut up."

"You want to get some breakfast?" He started the truck, heading back toward the main road. "You'll feel better if you eat."

That was debatable. Right now, all she wanted was to crawl into a hole and never surface again. "Are you sure you want to be seen with me?"

He laughed. "Aw, sugar. You might have been a little bit of a shit show last night, but trust me—I've seen worse. I've *been* worse."

That was strangely comforting. "I should know better. I'm not twenty-one. Four shots in half an hour is more than enough to make me act a fool." She crossed her arms over her chest and slumped down. "I hate that he makes me so crazy. That they *all* make me so crazy. Everyone thinks that I've accomplished all I'm going to in life—that I had my chance at greatness and Grant and blew it—and they've written me off as a result." She should be past it by now, shouldn't she? But Grant showing back up in town was like rubbing salt in her wound. Every time she turned around, someone was giving her considering looks like they should be asking her if she was *really* okay. She'd walk to hell and back before her pinnacle in life was dating *that* man.

That said, the whole situation wasn't *all* bad.

There had been Adam, after all. Fake boyfriend or not, spending time with him wasn't exactly a hardship. *Assuming he's not going to drop me off on my front doorstep and hightail it out of town as far and fast as this rig can take him.* "I don't suppose you still want to have sex with me?"

"Sugar, come here."

She slid across the seat and yelped when he grabbed her hand and pressed it against the front of his jeans. His length met her touch, hard enough to make her bite her lip. Adam's eyes were dark as he looked into hers. "I'm always ready for you. If you think for a second getting a little drunk and trying to fight your ex is enough to make me change my mind about wanting you, you've got another think coming."

"Oh."

"All the words in the world and that's the one you respond with."

She could do better. Really, she could. Jules swallowed hard. "I'm glad. I like having sex with you."

Adam threw back his head and let loose a laugh that resonated with something in her chest. "Damn, sugar. You're something else—and before you go overthinking things, I mean that as a compliment."

Considering every other time someone had said something of that nature, they hadn't meant it as anything positive, she wasn't used to being complimented. "You are a strange, strange man, Adam Meyer."

"It's been said before." He turned onto the highway, heading away from Devil's Falls. There were a grand total of four towns within easy drivable distance, and the only one in this direction was Pecos, so they had a good thirty minutes before they got to wherever he was headed.

She settled against him. "I know this is like two weeks late, but you really aren't what I expected."

"Oh, yeah?"

She ignored the tight way he spoke. "You're such a… well, a good guy. From the way some of the locals talk about the legendary Adam Meyer, I expected a hell-raiser." People still talked about the time he started a brawl after the Devils' rivals beat them in the division championships. Yeah, he'd been all of seventeen at the time, but he'd gone on to be a freaking *bull* rider. Every rodeo cowboy she'd met over the years was a hard-core adrenaline junkie. Adam just seemed so…well, not chill exactly, but not like a junkie jonesing for his next hit. He was intense and sometimes he moved around a room like the walls were closing in, but he wasn't anything like she'd imagined.

And that wasn't even getting into the sex and how out-of-this-world good it'd been.

He still didn't say anything, so she just kept talking. "Do you like bull riding?"

"I love it." His hands tightened on the steering wheel. "Those few seconds are the only time everything around me becomes crystal clear and quiet. I feel fucking invincible."

"Before you're thrown butt over teakettle and have to run away because the bull is angry and looking for someone to take it out on."

He smiled. "Yeah, before then."

It felt almost like he was opening up to her, so she pushed her luck a little. "I hear you're something of a rodeo star."

"That's not why I do it."

She traced the veins in his forearm as he drove. "You must have a whole lot of stories that would scare years off your friends' lives."

"A few." There was that smile again, the one she was seriously starting to crave. "Down in San Antonio a few years back, there was this big, mean old brute by the name of Sue."

Jules blinked. "Sue. As in the song?"

"The very one." He chuckled softly. "Well, he has a nasty history of putting his riders in the hospital, to the point where the odds of hitting eight seconds is so far against them, a man can make a pretty penny if he manages."

There was no mistaking the self-satisfied tone of his voice. "You did it."

"I did it. I went eight point one seconds." His eyes went

a little distant. "It was one hell of a ride, sugar. There hasn't been any quite like it since." He glanced down at her, his smile fading. "I never told anyone back home about it. Mama would worry, and I don't like the boys to think I'm bragging."

There was something almost sad about that. He'd done some incredible things, and to not be able to share it with anyone... Jules snuggled closer to him, wishing she could soothe the faint ache she heard behind the surface happiness of his words. "How did you even get started on that? Was it something you were determined to do as a kid, with the added bonus of giving your mother gray hair?"

A terrible, hopeless expression passed over his face, but he was answering her before she could ask what had put it there. "It was never on my list. I actually had started working with your cousin on your uncle's farm before I graduated high school, and I liked it a lot."

If she thought picturing Adam on a bull was hotter than hot, picturing him on a horse and herding cattle was downright devastating. There was something so attractive about a man, rugged and a little dirty, working the land and animals. She looked away, trying to get a handle on her hormones. "Why'd you stop if you liked it so much?"

"Something just clicked inside me at graduation. It was like a whole new world of possibilities opened up, and I couldn't wait to get the hell out of Dodge." He hesitated. "Not going to lie, I considered coming back right around the time I hit twenty-one. Your uncle Rodger offered me a job, and the other guys were running things at the ranch. I came back to help out over the holidays, but..."

That was when John died.

She knew the story. Everyone in town did. How Adam, Quinn, Daniel, John, and John's little sister were on their way back into town when a truck swerved and hit them. John had been killed on impact, and his little sister had her leg horribly mangled.

Jules swallowed hard. "Losing him must have been awful." She knew her cousin had never quite recovered.

"It was." He was silent for a beat. "I lasted until his funeral, but then I started getting restless again. Since then, I haven't stayed in one place more than a week or two."

And they were topping out two right now.

Jules couldn't imagine it. She loved her family, loved her friends, just plain loved Devil's Falls. It was her home and it might be a pain occasionally, but the good far outweighed the bad. She understood needing a break, but Adam had started driving and never come back. "I bet you've seen some cool stuff in all your traveling, though."

"Yeah. There are places where you can drive for miles and miles without seeing another person. Sometimes I camp out in the truck under the open sky and just…am. And the rodeo is something else. The energy is off the charts, amping up the people, which amps up the animals. It's a show unlike any other."

She'd only been a few times, and the last time, she'd seen one of the bull riders get trampled. He'd fallen after a great ride and while everyone was cheering, he hadn't gotten up fast enough and the bull had done a number on him. He lived, but he'd never ride again.

The thought of that happening to Adam…

Jules did her best to think of *anything* else. "But you're back in town for your mom—because she's sick."

"Yeah."

Even after the short time they'd known each other, she recognized his tone of voice. He was shutting her out. Again. It shouldn't hurt. She had no right to the information. She wasn't *really* his girlfriend.

And he's not staying.

She *had* to remember that, to keep it in the forefront of her mind. To do anything else was emotional suicide.

Chapter Fifteen

Jules shut the door softly behind her and turned the lock. She inched backward, skirting the floorboard that creaked...and screamed.

"Where were you?" Aubry sat on the couch, wrapped up in a blanket like a burrito, only her face and hands showing. She peered at Jules through bloodshot amber eyes. "You left your phone here."

"I know. I'm sorry. I didn't plan to be out this long." She plopped down on the couch next to her. "Have you been up all night?"

Aubry shrugged. "There was a new map pack on my game. And then you didn't come home, so I figured I'd just keep playing."

Her friend had always loved gaming, but this was a lot, even for her. *I'm a horrible person. She was worried about me and I was getting drunk and passing out.* She should have borrowed Adam's phone and called. "You want to go get some breakfast?"

"Already on it. Johnny Jacob is bringing me the breakfast

special from the Finer Diner."

She blinked. "I didn't realize Finer Diner delivered." Probably because they *didn't* in the twenty-six years she'd lived in this town. "Is that a new thing?"

"Not officially." Aubry leaned back with a sigh and set her controller aside. "I didn't feel like dealing with people, and cooking is for savages."

"You just think that because you could burn water."

"Details, details." She waved that away. "I'm tipping him twenty bucks, but it's worth it to avoid going down to the diner." She shuddered. "People see me sitting alone and think that it's sad and I look lonely, and they sit down and talk and, worse, they expect me to talk back."

"You poor thing." She patted her head. There was a knock on the door, and she hopped up to get it. There was a wad of cash in the frog mug by the door and she grabbed that on her way. Johnny Jacob smiled when she opened the door. "Hey, Jules!"

"Johnny." She passed over the cash. "You're up early."

He was starting to come out of that awful stage of puberty where the body seemed determined to go through as many awkward changes as possible in a seriously short amount of time. He was still breaking out and gangly to the point where she wanted to feed him a cheeseburger or twelve, but now there were hints of the man he'd be. *Where the heck did the time go?*

He grinned. "I picked up a second job for the rest of the summer. I've got my eye on that sweet little Ford for sale down on Upriver Drive."

"Good for you." She took the plastic bags from him. "You have a nice day now."

"You, too." He stopped at the top of the stairs. "Hey. Is it true that you're dating Adam Meyer?"

Apparently the plan was working. She didn't know if she

found that comforting or just exhausting, especially after this morning. "Yep."

His face lit up. "That's so *cool*. Did you know he rides bulls? He's held the record down at San Antonio for seven years." There was a fair amount of hero worship on his face, and she couldn't blame him. Adam really was larger than life. There was a lot he'd done that was insanely cool, whether to a teenage boy or a twenty-six-year-old cat café owner.

I like him. Crap.

"He's pretty great."

"He's *the best*. If I wasn't going to college, I'd totally be a bull rider. I bet he gets mad chicks." He flushed beet red. "Er, sorry, Jules. I didn't mean anything by it. I just—"

"It's okay. I'll see you around." She eased the door shut, her good mood slipping away. Because Johnny Jacob was right—Adam Meyer was like catnip to women. He might not have put that power to use since he'd been back in Devil's Falls—probably because *she'd* jumped him the first time he was out and about—but that didn't change the fact that he'd probably left a string of broken hearts behind him.

She set the food down in front of Aubry on the coffee table and resumed her seat. "Why does it bother me that Adam may have banged his way through half of Texas?"

"Because you like him." Aubry took out the foam containers and set them in a neat little row. "But you know you're not really dating and that this thing is ending at some point, so you don't have the security of being able to discount his past."

That was it exactly. Jules sighed. "Pretending to date him was a mistake." Especially when it had become clear that they couldn't keep their hands off each other.

"Then we don't you date him for real?"

She frowned as Aubry nudged a container over to her. "For me?" She opened it. "Holy crap, you got me French toast with blueberry syrup. How'd you know I'd be back in time?" It didn't matter that she'd just eaten with Adam. There was always room for French toast with blueberry syrup.

"I had a feeling." Aubry smiled her Cheshire cat smile. "Now, back to your clusterfuck of a love life…"

"I love you, but you kind of suck at pep talks." She cut up the French toast and doused it in the syrup. "I can't date him for real. That's not what he agreed to, and if I suddenly pull something like that, he's going to freak out. Aubry, I can't even ask him if he's okay without him shutting me down. The man has more issues than *Vogue*."

Aubry made a sound suspiciously like a moan at her first bite of omelet. "I'd think you're used to it after dealing with me all these years. You're an old pro at people with issues."

It was true that her friend had some…triggers. And hated people. And would hole up in their apartment for weeks on end if left to her own devices. She chewed, closing her eyes in pure bliss. "That's different."

"Not really. I don't know if you've noticed, but Adam has a ring of space around him wherever he goes." She took another bite. "I wish he'd teach me how to do that. I go out and randos come up and tell me that they'll pray for me or to keep my chin up because it can't be *that* bad. This?" She pointed at herself. "This is my face. This is the way it looks."

Jules had never really thought about it, but Adam *did* kind of have a don't-screw-with-me vibe. "He's just gone through a lot."

"We all have. There's no reason not to date him for real if he's making you all twitterpated."

She ate half her French toast before she responded. "What if he says he doesn't want to date me? He's not staying in Devil's Falls. He's made *that* abundantly clear."

"Look, Jules, I'm going to be honest with you." Aubry set her food aside and rotated to face her, her expression solemn.

"There's only room in this relationship for one paranoid, antisocial, budding agoraphobic. That's me. You're the bright and sunny one that makes people smile just by walking into the room. You're my better half. Maybe you could be his better half, too."

Jules leaned back and stared at the ceiling. "When did you get so smart?"

"I'm really good at diagnosing other people's problems. Mine? Not so much." Aubry went back to eating. "Now, finish your food and go shower. You smell like a bar."

Chapter Sixteen

It had been too long since Adam was on the back of a horse. So when Daniel mentioned that he needed some extra help around the ranch, he'd jumped at the opportunity. He'd been driving himself, his mama, *and* Lenora crazy being cooped up in the house, and she'd practically shoved him through the door the second his friend called.

He just hadn't expected Daniel to saddle him up a stallion named Hellbeast. He stared at the giant animal. The horse was gorgeous, standing at seventeen hands and perfectly shaped. He was a glossy chestnut with white stockings, looking more suited to the show ring than cattle herding. "Hellbeast."

"You heard right." Daniel finished cinching the saddle on his bay. "He's not as bad as he seems."

Adam took a step closer and stopped when Hellbeast snorted. "Really?"

"Yep." His friend grinned. "He's worse."

"This wouldn't be you getting me back for fake dating your cousin, would it?" He took the reins and moved forward. The best path with any foul-tempered animal was to show no hesitation. He had a feeling the second Hellbeast scented fear, he'd take off for the horizon, whether he kept his rider on his back or not.

"Would I do that?"

He swung up into the saddle, holding the horn when Hellbeast sidled sideways. "Yes."

"He likes to try to jump the south fence, so watch out for that."

Adam shot him a look. "I know you're pissed, but murder seems like an overreaction."

"Murder?" Daniel shook his head. "You're Adam Meyer, famous bull rider. If anyone can handle little ole Pumpernickel, it's you."

"I thought you said his name was Hellbeast."

They started away from the barn. The stallion kept a tight trot, his stride liquid and absolutely perfect. Daniel adjusted his cowboy hat. "That's just what I call him, though don't do it in Jules's hearing. She's got a soft spot for the beast."

Of course she did. He'd bet *Pumpernickel* adored her, too. She was the kind of woman who could sing the birds from the trees and charm everyone she came across. Except maybe Grant. The thought soured his mood. The more he thought about her with that jackass, the more it bothered him. What the hell had she been thinking, dating a guy like that? He was human waste.

And maybe Adam was fucking jealous.

They rode south along the fence line. The job today was mending fence posts. It was tedious work, but by lunchtime, he'd worked hard enough that his muscles burned pleasantly and his thoughts were clear for the first time in what felt like forever. He stretched, his back popping.

"You know there's a place here if you decide to stay."

He didn't look at Daniel. His friend, of all people, should know why he couldn't stay. The fact that he'd stuck around long enough to see graduation was a small miracle. As his mama often reminded him, he was a leaver, same as his daddy.

"I get wanting to leave this place in your rearview. Believe me, I do. But…" Daniel trailed off. "I don't know why I'm trying to convince you. I have half a mind to take a page from your book and move away for good."

Before he could ask what his friend meant, the sound of hoofbeats had them both turning. A figure raced across the open field, crouched over the back of a dark horse. She pulled up with a few short feet to spare, grinning down at them from beneath her wide-brimmed hat. "Howdy, fellas."

Adam couldn't stop staring. He'd spared a thought to what Jules might look like on the back of a horse, but seeing her in a faded black tank top and jeans whose fit could only be described a lovingly clingy made his brain short-circuit. She handled herself like she'd been born in the saddle — something he should have considered with Daniel being her cousin and all. "Jules."

"I brought you guys lunch." She shrugged out of a backpack he hadn't seen before then. "Hope you like ham and cheese, Adam. It's Daniel's favorite, and Aunt Lori is feeling generous."

"Probably buttering me up to set me up with a daughter of some friend of hers," Daniel grumbled, taking the bag from her.

Adam didn't miss the worry that clouded her expression. Everyone seemed to be worried about Daniel. He turned to look at his friend. The man seemed moodier than he had been twelve years ago, and he couldn't help thinking about what Quinn had said at the bonfire about John's death changing Daniel fundamentally. Crippling guilt would do that to a person.

The man in question grabbed a plastic container from the backpack. "Thanks, kid. I'm going to go check the posts farther down." He untethered his bay and swung up into the saddle. And then he was gone, cantering away.

Jules's feet hit the ground, and she walked her horse over to loop the reins around the fence. "You boys sure do have the market cornered on brooding, don't you?"

"Don't know what you're talking about."

She scooped up the backpack. "Of course you don't. You're just a little ray of sunshine."

"Yep." They sat next to the fence, and he accepted the sandwich and baggie full of chips. In the winter, lunch would be a sandwich and a canteen of soup—probably chicken noodle or tomato. He unwrapped his ham and cheese and took a bite, hit by a wave of homesickness that threatened to take him out at the knees. It didn't make sense. He *was* home.

But not for good.

Will I even be *here in the winter?*

He set the sandwich down and leaned back against the post he'd fixed earlier, his appetite gone. Some days he'd go through an entire day without having to face that fact that his mama was fading away before his eyes. And then it'd hit like a lightning strike, charring him to the bone. "She's got cancer, you know."

Jules froze. "I'm sorry."

It said something that she didn't ask whom he was talking about. She knew his mom was sick. Fuck, everyone in this godforsaken town knew his mom was sick—and probably had known before he did. He'd failed her in so many ways. Even knowing there wasn't a damn thing he could do about her cancer, he couldn't shake the feeling that he was failing her now, too. "I should have been here." He didn't know why he was saying this shit aloud, let alone to Jules. She'd signed on for the fun side of the girlfriend experience, not the baggage that came with it.

"I don't know if it'll make you feel better or worse to

know it, but she hid it for a very long time, even from her lady friend, Lenora. They come into my shop every week, and I knew she looked a little peaky, but she just said she wasn't sleeping well. Even if you'd been here, I doubt she would have told you until she was forced to."

She was probably right, but that didn't make it any easier to bear. "But I would have *been* here."

"You're here now."

"Yeah, I guess I am." He forced himself to pick his sandwich back up and take another bite. He'd need the calories to finish out the day, whether he was hungry or not. "So, what are you doing out here?"

"Oh, me? I usually help out on my days off when there isn't something that I need to be doing for Cups and Kittens." She took a long drink of water. "And I might have known you were out here, so I volunteered to bring you guys lunch."

He smiled. "Now the truth comes out."

"Guilty." She twisted a strand of her dark hair around her finger. "I wanted to talk to you about something, but in the light of everything, I think it was a horrible Aubry-induced idea."

Color him crazy, but any idea that came from that redhead made him curious. "Tell me."

"I'd really rather not." She huffed out a breath when he leveled a look at her. "Okay, fine. Do you want to be my boyfriend for real?"

He'd anticipated all sorts of words to come out of her mouth…but not that. "You want to date me."

"I know we're already sort of dating, but it's fake dating. I want to real date." She scrunched up her nose when she frowned. "Though, to be honest, I don't really know what would be different. Maybe more sex? Or you tell me what's wrong when I ask if you're okay?"

"Sugar—"

"You're not staying. I know." Her smile was all sorts of tentative. "But you haven't left yet. I like you, Adam. And I think you like me, too."

Hell, yes, he did. Too much. Jules wasn't the leaving kind. She was the type of woman that had a man thinking all sorts of insane thoughts about settling down and kids and coming in from work to find the windows lit and dinner on the stove. The kind of woman who had "home" written all over her.

You'll break her heart if you say yes. Maybe not today, maybe not tomorrow, but it's coming.

But not today.

He pulled her into his lap. "Well, fuck, sugar, you make one hell of an argument."

Her hands landed on his shoulders. "Is that a no?"

"Nope." He ran his hands up her thighs. "These jeans should be fucking illegal."

"What? These are work jeans." She frowned. "You didn't really answer my question."

"Sure I did. Yes, sugar, be my girlfriend." *Until I leave Devil's Falls in my rearview once and for all.* He dipped his thumbs beneath her waistband. "Now let me get you out of these jeans."

She laughed and slapped his hands. "Daniel's going to be back any time, and as much as I want to jump your bones, I'd rather not have to pay for the therapy he'd inevitably need if he saw us bumping uglies."

"Jump my bones? Bumping uglies? I don't think my dirty-talking lessons have had their desired effect. We'll need a repeat."

She leaned forward until her lips brushed his ear. "Come by when you get off work. I'll be waiting for you with nothing but a sheet on."

"Lose the sheet and you've got yourself a deal."

Jules laughed, though the sound turned into a moan when

he used his grip on her hips to slide her against the hard ridge of his cock. "Maybe I'll be wearing panties and cowgirl boots. Or these jeans and nothing else. You'll have to show up to find out."

He cursed low and hard. "I'm going to be in hell for the rest of the day. I hope you're happy."

She pressed a quick kiss to his lips and wriggled free. "I am."

And hell if she didn't sound it.

Chapter Seventeen

Jules paced from one side of her apartment to the other. *This was such a dumb idea. What if he doesn't show up. Worse, what if he does?* She looked down at her getup—boots and panties and a long-sleeved flannel shirt that she'd left unbuttoned. When she got dressed, she'd had that look on Adam's face fixated in her mind. He would have had her right then and there in the field without a second thought.

But that was the problem. He'd had the entire afternoon for second thoughts. It didn't matter if he'd said he was coming over and that he'd be her boyfriend for real—he could have changed his mind.

She eyed the closed door to Aubry's room. Her friend had taken one look at her, shaken her head, and gone off to hide. Not that Jules could blame her—she felt a whole lot like hiding right now, too.

A knock on the door had her considering diving for the thick, knitted throw blanket on the back of the couch. What had she been thinking, dressing like this? She looked like one of those cowgirl wannabes in a music video. It didn't help that her boots, having seen better days, probably ruined the effect. They were the boots of a woman who *worked*.

She started to kick them off, but whoever it was at the door knocked again. Jules hurried over and peered through the peephole. *Adam.* There was no way he didn't know she was here—especially since *she'd* been the one to tell him she would be. She rested her forehead against the door. "Get it together, Jules."

"Sugar, if you're going to talk to yourself, you might as well let me in so you can talk to me instead."

Her eyes flew open. "Sorry, but I think I'm going to die of embarrassment."

"Let me in." His voice turned coaxing. "Do you know how I spent the rest of my day?"

It was strange having this conversation through the door, but she didn't immediately move. "How?"

"Hard as a rock and aching for you. Let me in, and I'll tell you all about it."

She opened the door to find him grinning. "Said the big bad wolf to the little pig."

The expression melted away as he took her in. Adam's eyes went dark, and he rubbed a hand across his mouth. "Fuck, sugar, I changed my mind. I'm not going to tell you a damn thing. I'm going to show you." He cleared the doorway in a single step, backing her into the apartment and kicking the door shut behind him. "The redhead?"

"She has a name." Jules took several steps back, her heart beating too hard.

"I know." He shadowed her movements, following her as she backed around the kitchen table and toward her bedroom.

"She's in her room."

He passed the doorway into her room and kicked it shut behind him, too. "Then you better be quiet or we're going to traumatize the hell out of her."

"Keep—" She shrieked when he burst around the corner of the bed and scooped her into his arms. Jules braced herself, but he didn't throw her onto the bed this time. Instead he laid her down and sat back, looking at her like... She didn't have words to describe how he was looking at her.

He smoothed his hands up her legs, spreading them as he reached her thighs. "Fuck, sugar." His thumb played down and stroked over her panties. "Wet, just like I knew you'd be."

"I guess I like being chased."

His expression was nearly pained. "That's good. I like the fuck out of chasing you." He hooked the sides of her panties and dragged them down her legs. "One of these days, I'm going to set you loose in a field in nothing but these boots. And then I'm going to chase you down and fuck you right there in the grass."

It was suddenly a whole lot harder to draw a full breath. She could picture it perfectly, that hungry look on his face as he stalked after her, the wheat whipping at her legs, her body exposed to the breeze.

"You like that. Good." He got her panties past her boots and tossed them to the side. "Spread your legs, sugar. Show me how much you want me."

She did what he said, feeling a little foolish, but that feeling faded as he started talking. "Did your little tease act this afternoon leave you as worked up as it did me?"

"Yes."

"Mmm." He gripped her thighs, spreading her wider yet. "And did you come home and get one of those little buzzy toys out?"

How did he know?

He must have read something on her face. "You're far too relaxed to have spent the last few hours like I did."

A blush spread across her cheeks. "I've come three times since I got home."

He froze, his eyes narrowed. "Three."

"Yes…"

"Three fucking orgasms you denied me." He yanked her to the edge of the bed as he went to his knees beside it. "Three orgasms that should have been mine."

"Well—" She had to slap a hand over her mouth when he licked up her center, zeroing in on her clit. She was already sensitive from all the orgasms earlier, and the pleasure was so acute, it was almost painful as he sucked her clit into his mouth. "*Adam.*"

"I'm taking what's mine, sugar. With interest."

He went at her like a starving man. There was no stopping, no passing Go, no collecting two hundred dollars. There was just an Adam-induced orgasm hurtling down on her. She grabbed her comforter and screamed her pleasure into it, writhing against his mouth.

But he wasn't done. He was nowhere near done.

The aftershocks had barely faded when he flipped her onto her stomach. "That's one."

Surely he didn't really mean to…

His hand cupped her, sliding through her wetness, two fingers spearing her and then withdrawing to slide over her oversensitive clit. Over and over again. With her butt in the air and her face pressed against her mattress, she should have felt horribly exposed, but there was no room for feeling anything but what he was doing to her. An impossible pressure built in her, spiraling higher and higher with each stroke. "Adam, please."

"Did you think of me when you were rubbing that vibrator all over your clit? I think you did. I think you knew exactly how hard I was for you, and that only got you off harder knowing that I was riding around with a cockstand to end all cockstands."

It *had* felt naughty to be pleasuring herself while she knew he wasn't able to. She moaned, trying to thrust back onto his fingers, but he slapped her butt hard enough to sting. "Hold still, sugar. This is my rodeo, and you've got to pay your dues."

"You're so mean."

"You have no idea." He pinched her clit, the shock of the pain sending her hurtling into another orgasm. Jules collapsed onto her bed, her legs shaking and her breath coming so hard, she sounded like she'd just run a marathon.

He rolled her onto her back. "Breathe, sugar."

"I'm…breathing." Sort of.

Adam licked between her legs again, but the earlier fury driving him seemed to be at least partially abated because he took his time as if savoring the taste of her. She lay there, half sure she was having an out-of-body experience. It was the only explanation for her wanting to grab his hair and grind herself against his face even after two orgasms in entirely too little time.

She stretched her arms over her head, arching her back. "You make me crazy."

"Believe me, the feeling is fucking mutual." He spread her folds, fucking her with his tongue the same way he'd fucked her with his fingers. It made her feel sexy and wanton and like someone else entirely.

"*Adam.*"

"That's right, sugar. Me. Not your fucking buzzy toy." He lifted his head, something dangerous flickering over his face. "Where is it?"

She pointed to her nightstand before common sense caught up with her. "Wait—" But it was too late. He'd yanked open the drawer and brought out B.O.B.

Adam eyed the bright pink Lelo vibrator. "Interesting taste." He turned it on, a wicked grin spreading over his face. "On second thought, I think your buzzy toy and I would make a fucking amazing tag team." He slid the vibrator into her, adjusting the setting until she had to fist the comforter over her head.

"Oh my God."

"One more orgasm, and I'll let you come on my cock." He fucked her slowly with the vibrator. The sensation of his hands on her body, combined with the toy between her legs, made the pleasure almost impossible to bear. "That's it, sugar. Let go. I've got you."

He lined it up with her clit, squeezing her thigh with his free hand. "You look so fucking beautiful when you come. Knowing I'm the cause of it… Yeah, I can't get enough of that. I'm going to fuck that tight pussy of yours, sugar, until you're begging me to never stop."

Considering how close she was to doing just that, she believed him with every fiber of her being. She shuddered, her orgasm looming.

Which was when he took away her vibrator. She barely had time to protest when he was there, covering her, his cock replacing the buzzy toy. The feeling of him filling her sent her over the edge. Jules buried her face against his neck and sobbed as she came, his hands on her and his cock inside her the only solid thing in her world in that moment.

He slipped one arm beneath the small of her back and the other hand cupped the back of her head as he thrust into her, his mouth on hers, his tongue fucking her as thoroughly as his cock. The sensation was too much, forcing her orgasm to crest again. This time, he followed her over, his strokes becoming less smooth and his body going tight on top of her as he groaned her name.

She lay there, staring at her ceiling, wondering if this was all a dream. Surely the single sexiest man she'd ever known hadn't just made her come three times in short order. That was just too good to be true.

And then Adam had to go and make it even better. He turned his head and kissed her neck. "Sugar, I'm going to take you on a real date."

Chapter Eighteen

Adam scrubbed his truck down, wondering what the hell he'd been thinking yesterday with Jules. *I'm going to take you on a real date. I'll be your boyfriend.* He was setting himself up for failure. "I'm *not staying*, goddamn it."

"Are you talking to yourself?"

He glanced over to find Quinn standing at the bottom of his mom's driveway. "What are you doing here?"

"So damn rude." His friend shook his head. "But I know what you really meant to say." He grinned and waved, his voice ticking up an octave. "'Hey, man, nice to see you. It's been a hell of a week and your gorgeous face is exactly what I needed.'"

Adam shook his head. "No, pretty sure that's not what I meant at all. And I don't sound like that."

"Sure you do." He settled into the rocking chair on the porch, absolutely dwarfing the thin wood with his large body. "You still doing that thing with Daniel's cousin? Because rumor has it that you were seen making out like high school kids on her front doorstep yesterday in the early hours of the morning."

"Rumor has it, huh? This town never changes."

Growing up, more often than not, it'd been his name uttered as the hell-raiser who couldn't keep himself out of the back of the town's lone police cruiser. It wasn't anything personal—there just wasn't a whole hell of a lot to talk about other than football, ranching, and who was getting into trouble this week.

"Sure, it changes. Just ask my old man." Quinn deepened his voice and screwed up his face in a scowl. "'Back in my day, we respected our country and didn't act like damn fools.'"

"You are seriously god-awful at impressions." Adam chuckled. "How's Sir Charles, anyways? He made his peace with you working with Daniel instead of heading up his oil empire yet?"

"Hardly." Quinn stretched his legs out and laced his fingers behind his head. "If anything, he's getting more desperate to bring me back into the fold. At the obligatory family dinner last month, he invited *two* blondes with tits the size of melons and dollar signs in their eyes. Mother was thrilled. Naturally."

"Naturally." He crouched down and went to work on his wheels. When he was a teenager, he'd envied the fact that Quinn's dad was determined to have him follow in his footsteps. Once he hit his early twenties, though, he recognized it for the ball and chain it was. Charles Baldwyn cared less about his son's happiness than he did about continuing his family traditions. Adam still wasn't sure if an overbearing ass of a dad was better than no dad at all, but he'd stopped envying his friend. "How long did he manage to go without offering one of them up in marriage?"

"A whole hour." Quinn sighed. "You'd think they'd be bothered by him dangling them in front of me like a piece of meat, but they didn't so much as blink."

"Money makes people stupid."

"Isn't that the truth?" He crossed his feet at his ankles. "That was a nice subject change—very subtle. But you still didn't answer my question about little Jules Rodriguez."

He didn't want to get into it. He could fool himself into thinking this wasn't going to end in a complete train wreck—mostly—but Quinn would have no problem calling him out. "I don't want to talk about it."

Quinn dropped his hands and sat up straight. "What the hell is going on with you and that girl?"

"She's only seven years younger than us. It's not like I'm robbing the fucking cradle."

If anything, his friend just looked *more* interested. "See, that's the thing. I thought you guys were playing a game—you do her a favor and make that asshole ex of hers jealous, and she occupies you so you don't drive your mom insane pacing around the house. But that's not what it sounds like when you say stuff like that. Are you actually interested in her?"

Yes. He pushed to his feet and grabbed the hose, spraying down the truck. "It's not like that."

"Are you sure?"

Adam didn't say anything until he'd finished washing off the truck and disposed of the soapy water in the bucket. "You know she's just using me to create a scandal."

"And?"

He sighed and turned to face his friend. "And that's a temporary thing no matter which way you look at it. She doesn't want to settle down with the hell-raiser who gets the gossip mill raging. She wants the slow and steady guy who's going to be there with her every night and making her coffee and shit in the morning and…" He rubbed a hand over his face. "It's not me. That's never going to be me."

"Yeah, you keep saying that. Maybe you just haven't found a good enough reason to put down roots and be that guy—until now."

That's what he was afraid of. Not that he'd put down roots, but that he'd start to and then the restlessness in his blood would start up again. He'd turn back into a tumbleweed before a gale-force wind, yanked right out of whatever life he thought he could have here.

And, really, what did he have to offer Jules? He was a few years out of being a washed-up bull rider who'd been lucky enough not to be permanently injured but who didn't exactly have any applicable skills otherwise. The thought tightened his throat. Rationally, he knew he couldn't ride bulls forever, but he didn't have any long-term plans beyond working the rodeo in whatever capacity he could. Which was pathetic when he really sat down to think about it.

And his mama…

"I'm not that man." He said it more firmly, as if that could quell the growing thing in his chest that was determined to take on a life of its own. It was all twisted up with his dread about what might happen to his mama, a weird mix of fear and hope and something else that he had no name for. He tried to smile. "You know me — I am what I am."

"Sure — before. But you've been back in town almost three weeks now, and you're not going insane or fleeing at the first chance you get." He motioned at the truck. "Hell, you're downright respectable these days."

His gave his front door a long look. "I have my reasons. They aren't permanent."

"Sounds like you have more than one these days." Quinn held up his hands when Adam glared. "Sorry, sorry. Can't help that I miss you when you're off living life like a country song."

"For fuck's sake." Adam ducked into the garage and grabbed two beers. He walked back, dropped into the chair next to his friend, and passed one over. "You're ridiculous."

"It should be my middle name." Quinn took a long drink of his beer. "So why are you getting your ride all shined up?"

He didn't want to admit it, but his friend would pester him if he tried to avoid the topic. "I'm taking Jules out on a real date."

Quinn threw back his head and let loose a booming laugh. "Oh God, that's the funniest shit I've heard all day. Sounds like you're doing a hell of a job of keeping things in perspective with her."

"Something like that." He was doing such a good job, he'd gone from pretending to date her to actually dating her. He took a deep breath and turned the conversation, grateful when Quinn allowed it this time. They chatted about cattle and Adam told a few of his wild rodeo stories, and before he knew it, it was time to go pick up Jules.

His friend stopped by the driver's door and Adam rolled down the window. The joking expression on Quinn's face dropped for the first time since he'd shown up. "Daniel's cousin is a good girl."

"Are you fucking kidding me?" He expected this from his mom and the townsfolk in general—it even made sense for Daniel to be warning him off since Jules was *his* cousin. To have Quinn doing it, too…it stung. A lot. "I'm not stringing her along. I've been honest with her from the beginning, and she's been with me every step of the way. Jules is a grown-ass woman, and I doubt she'd take kindly to everyone and their dog being so sure that I'm going to break her heart."

Quinn raised his eyebrows. "Touched on a sore spot, didn't I?"

"I get tired of everyone thinking I'm a piece of shit." Even if he agreed with them most days.

"Nobody thinks that—or at least no one worth mentioning." He shook his head. "All I was going to say, jackass, is that I think she might be good for you." He turned around and walked off without another word, leaving Adam staring after him.

He'd done a *spectacular* job of proving to his friend that he was managing to keep calm and rational about this situation. He headed for Jules's place, kicking himself again for letting what everyone else thought of him get under his skin. She knew the score. Fuck, *she* was the one with a future that didn't fit him in the least. She'd be a fool to let her heart get involved.

Except she asked you to be her boyfriend. And you said yes.

It didn't mean anything—not really. Even if they were dating for real—which wasn't that different from them pretending to date—she knew he was leaving. He knew he was leaving. The entire fucking town knew he was leaving. It'd be fun while it lasted, but it *couldn't* last.

He stopped in front of her café, shut off the engine, and headed inside, still arguing with himself. He wasn't some monster, taking advantage of little innocent Jules Rodriguez. *She'd* come to *him. She* was the one who wanted sex. Yeah, he'd taken them all the way up to that point, but she'd pushed them over the edge.

If anything, people should be worried about how *he* was going to take the goddamn breakup. He'd never been with a woman like this before—someone who seemed to bring joy into any room she stepped into, someone who always had a new and wacky perspective on life, someone who was *happy*. Grant might have set her on her heels temporarily, but that wouldn't last. Jules was the type who bounced back, better than ever, and she would this time, too.

Just like she would after he left.

It was *Adam* who wasn't sure how the hell he was going to go back to life on the road after he'd known what it was like to hold her in his arms.

Chapter Nineteen

Jules walked out of the kitchen to find Adam standing in the doorway of her café, glaring down at the trio of cats twining around his feet. She eyed them—Cujo, Rick, and Dog—wondering if they'd done something to deserve the look. With those three, there was no telling. They got into more trouble than the rest of the cats combined. But Adam didn't seem to be bleeding and there were no suspicious wet spots on his pant legs—talking down Mr. Lee the last time *that* had happened had taken all of her not inconsiderable persuasive skills—so she was almost afraid to ask what was wrong.

Oh, right, I shouldn't even do it anyways, because he gets so freaking snarly about it.

So she pasted a smile on her face. "Hey, there."

He looked up, and the scowl disappeared. Jules actually rocked back on her heels. *Good lord, being smiled at by Adam Meyer is as good as one of those purple nurple shots. Better, even.* Adam carefully stepped over the cats and stalked toward her. "Hey, sugar."

She barely had a chance to process his intent before he

pulled her into his arms and kissed her. His lips brushed hers, which should have been PG, but one of his hands was at the small of her back, pressing her fully against the front of his *very* aroused body, and the other was in her hair, tugging hard enough that she knew exactly who was in charge of this encounter. Her toes curled in her boots, and she went all soft and melty. When he lifted his head, all she could do was blink up at him. "Hi."

His grin was so self-satisfied that her toes curled all over again. "You said that already."

"Did I? I think I'm in danger of saying it a third time." She clamped her mouth shut before she could do just that.

He leaned back a little. "You ready for our date?"

"Yes...don't I look ready?" She glanced down at herself. She'd chosen a dress from Aubry's closet that was a mash-up of pinup and country girl—in that it was plaid, which was as country girl as Aubry got. Jules had picked it because it was fancier than anything she owned, and it seemed like she should get fancy for a *real* date with Adam.

"You look good enough to eat."

"I hope you mean that in a non–Hannibal Lecter way, or I'm going to have to call the police," Aubry called out.

They both looked over to where Aubry sat in her usual corner seat with Mr. Winkles in her lap, a cup of coffee in her hands despite the fact that it was well after five in the evening. She speared Adam with a glare over the top of her glasses that would have had a lesser man hightailing it for the door.

Adam just grinned. "I mean it in a flirting way that has nothing to do with cannibalism."

She glared even harder. "I'm onto you, country boy. Treat my friend right."

Some of the humor fled his face, but his smile didn't waver. "Sure thing." He turned back to Jules and offered his elbow. "Do you need to do anything else before we go?"

She was as prepared as she was going to be. Aunt Lori was watching the café until her cousin Jamie showed up to finish off the shift and close. She crouched down carefully to give each of the cats at Adam's feet a scratch, though Cujo dodged her reach and leaped onto the counter to get closer to his face. *Thanks a lot, you silly thing.* She pushed to her feet and looked around. There were half a dozen other things she could find to occupy herself before they left, but anything else she would be stalling. "I think I'm good."

"Then let's get out of here."

They headed out onto the street, and she stopped short at the sight of his truck. It shone brightly in the evening sun, free of any dirt or dust or mud. "You cleaned your truck."

"My mama taught me that you don't pick up a lady in a filthy truck." He opened the door for her, looking as out of place as she suddenly felt.

Jules climbed up, wondering at the awkward feeling coursing through her body and making her want to fidget. This was a date. A *real* date. It shouldn't be any different than any of their other dates. She'd never had a problem speaking her mind with Adam, so why was she just staring at him mutely as he started his truck and headed down the road?

The minutes ticked by, the silence only getting stranger as time went on. They hit the town limits, and Jules was ready to scream. "Why is this so weird? We've been naked and in more compromising positions than I care to count and suddenly I feel like I'm sixteen and on my first date and don't know what to do with my hands."

Adam's hands flexed on the steering wheel. "I don't know."

She waited, but he didn't say anything else. There had to be some way to fix this, because the thought that she'd ruined them by changing things made her sick to her stomach. It was bad enough that he was leaving town at some unknown date in the future and that she'd likely never see him again—for this to end *before* he left? No. Absolutely not. She craved him like her favorite blanket and wine and B.O.B. all rolled into one. Except he could hold down a conversation and he really listened to her. Usually.

She had to do something, and she had to do it now.

Holding her breath, Jules slid across the bench seat until she was pressed against Adam from shoulder to knee. He took the hint and lifted his arm to rest it on the back of the seat. It wasn't putting his arm around her, but it'd have to do for now.

You can do this. You're in charge of your own destiny. You're bold and fearless and oh my God, I can't believe I'm doing this.

Before she could talk herself out of it, she went for his zipper.

Adam tensed. "Sugar, what do you think you're doing?"

"I'm being scandalous." She unbuttoned the top of his jeans and dragged his zipper down. "Stop talking before I chicken out."

"Chicken out from— *Holy shit.*"

She took him in her hand, almost breathing a sigh of relief when he grew hard. This, at least, hadn't changed. "I liked how things were between us. I don't want them to change."

"Do you think now is really the time for this conversation?"

Yes, because it was easier to put herself out there when she knew she had him at a slight disadvantage. She stroked him, using the motion she knew he liked. "I think it's the perfect time. I like you, Adam. I know that's silly, and I know you're leaving, and I know I can't ever ask you if you're okay, but I don't care. I want to enjoy the time we have, and we can't do that if we're sitting here not talking."

Adam pulled onto the shoulder and put the truck in park. "You have my full attention."

"Oh, well, good." She kept touching him, suddenly not sure where she wanted to take this. *Liar. You knew exactly what you wanted from the moment you decided to go for it.* With that little voice in her head driving her on, she kissed him.

Adam took control of the kiss immediately, gripping the back of her neck with one hand and angling his body so she could keep stroking him. "You are something else, sugar."

"You keep saying that. I keep taking it as a compliment."

"Good."

He reached down and hooked her knee, bringing her up and over to straddle him. It happened so smoothly, she didn't lose her grip and was left staring at him. "Tell the truth—do you practice that move? Because no one should be that good naturally."

He laughed, the deep sound rumbling between them. "I'll never tell."

Which was as good as admitting that he had. She waited for that splinter of jealousy to dig deeper, but there was nothing there. Who cared about his past—or his future, for that matter? Right now, in this moment, he was hers and hers alone. She kissed him again, wriggling closer, which hiked up her dress. He took the hint, running his hands up her legs to cup her butt and bring her down to line up the hard ridge of him against her clit.

She pulled away enough to say, "I want you inside me."

"You're reading my mind." He slid over to the middle of the seat and kept an arm around her waist as he fumbled in the glove compartment, coming up with a condom.

She eyed it. "How long has that been in there?" Weren't there some rules about keeping those things in a cool, dry place or risking them breaking? A glove compartment in Texas might be dry, but it sure wasn't cool.

"I put it in there this morning." He gave her a panty-melting smile. "Just call me optimistic."

"You're a scoundrel." She grabbed the condom from his hand. "I like it." It was quick work to rip the wrapper and roll the condom onto him. This was good. This, they knew how to do. The rest of it would fall into place once they had a chance to reset the clock.

Adam pulled her panties to the side, and she wasted no time sinking onto him. Jules closed her eyes, the feeling of fullness nearly overwhelming. She moved, taking him deeper. "This feels too good to be real."

"You took the words right out of my mouth." He unbuttoned the front of her dress and pushed it off her shoulders, taking her bra with it and baring her breasts. "Fuck, sugar, your body is a work of art." He let go of her hips to palm her breasts as she rode him. "You're so goddamn sexy, it makes me crazy. How the hell am I supposed to focus on anything else when every time I think about you, I can practically feel that tight little pussy of yours squeezing my cock?"

She gripped his shoulders and rolled her body, making him hit a spot inside her that had her moaning. "Sounds like a…personal problem."

"You have no fucking idea." He squeezed her breasts and then released them, the imprint of his hands burning itself into her memory. "And this?" He fisted the fabric of her dress, lifting it above her hips. "You sliding down my cock is a sight I could spend the rest of my life watching and never get tired of. Whoever made you feel like you were somehow less is a fucking idiot. You're perfect. You're better than perfect."

His words warmed her, even as her body sparked with the beginning of an orgasm. "Adam—"

"Need a little something to get you over the edge, don't you, sugar?" He grabbed her hip with one hand and slid his other down to stroke her clit. His grip guided her pace, taking the control from her even as his fingers took her exactly where she needed to go. Jules buried her face in his neck as she came, her shudders racking her entire body.

Adam laid her down on the seat, the position allowing him deeper. "Feeling you come around me, knowing that I'm the cause of it—there isn't another thing in this world like it." His voice went hoarse. "I've never had someone make me lose control like you do."

She clung to him as his strokes became more uneven, his hold on her tightening as he followed her over the edge, knowing that she was the cause of it making her entire body spark with pleasure all over again. "Adam, you're more addicting that nicotine."

"Oh, yeah?" His laugh rumbled through her. "I can't say I don't like hearing that."

She smiled, though the truth settled in her stomach. Nicotine might feel good in the moment, just like being with him did, but it was ultimately a toxic substance that only left pain in its wake.

Kind of like her relationship with Adam.

Chapter Twenty

Adam stared at his drink, feeling like a jackass. Jules had been right—things went weird as soon as they got into his truck. He'd known it, and he hadn't done a damn thing to stop it, not with Quinn's words still ringing in his ears, joining the chorus of everyone else who'd warned him away from her. Instead of making her comfortable, he'd let the silence draw on, punishing them both for thinking they could do this.

And then Jules had taken matters—and him—into her own hands. She was right—if there was one thing they knew how to do, it was have sex. They'd been doing just fine before becoming official and there was no reason anything had to change.

"You're thinking awfully hard over there."

He looked up to find Jules crossing her eyes at him. Adam laughed. "Life is never boring when you're around, is it?"

"On the contrary, most people think my life is incredibly boring. Or at least proceeding as expected." Her smile dimmed, but she seemed to make an effort to reclaim it. "But it's mine, and that's all anyone can really ask for, right? I like

Cups and Kittens and I like my best friend, even if she's a bit on the antisocial side, and I maybe I don't have a ton on the horizon when it comes to my love life, but I'm only twenty-six. I'm hardly a spinster that should just swear off the whole thing now—especially since we've been running around causing a ruckus. That's sure to open up some new avenues for me."

He started to point out that they were, in fact, on a date right now, but the truth slammed into his chest all over again. *I'm not what she wants.* He'd known it before—it was a truth he hadn't been able to escape from the very beginning—but somehow hearing her talk about potential prospects while sitting across the table from him made him sick to his stomach. He didn't want to think about her going out with another guy, or her sharing her goofy smiles with some other dude, or, fuck, her letting someone else between those sweet thighs.

"Adam?"

He realized he was clutching his cloth napkin in a white-knuckled grip. "Yeah, sorry." He had to get it together. He didn't have a goddamn right to be jealous of some future guy. He was here with her now, but he wouldn't be forever. That was *his* choice.

He just had to remember that.

"Why a cat café?"

She pressed her lips together but seemed to decide it wasn't worth asking him what the hell was going on in his head. Which was good, because he didn't fucking know. Jules took a sip of her water. "There have been quite a few studies done that show having a pet—any pet—is enough to combat everything from poor physical health to depression to plain old loneliness. Animals never ask for anything but love, and that's a gift that a lot of people don't have in their lives. But not everyone can have a pet of their own for various reasons—which is where I come in."

It was so...Jules. Loving and thoughtful and kind. "You

get a lot of traffic in there."

"Yep." She smiled. "Just being able to stop by, have a cup of coffee, and spend some time with a cat curled up in your lap is all some people need to restart their day. The cats love the attention. The people love the cats. And I love making people happy, so it's win-win across the board." She frowned. "Or win-win-win. Whatever. You know what I mean."

"I do." He'd always wanted a pet—though he was more inclined to dogs than cats—but his life made it hard to have one. There were other guys on the circuit who managed it, but to Adam, dogs represented stability. It wouldn't be right to have one without a yard or property to let him run free on. Being cooped up in the truck for hours on end, or tied to a fence while he rode…it would just be wrong.

"See. This is nice. We can hold down a conversation."

He chuckled. "And if the topics stall out, you can always slide on over here and offer up another solution."

Her face flamed red. "Shh, someone will hear you."

"I thought that was the whole point." He couldn't quite keep the irritation the thought brought out of his voice.

If anything, her blush got deeper. "That's was before. That's not what I want now."

Well, hell, he liked the sound of that. He looked around. El Pollo Delicioso was hardly five stars, but it had cloth napkins and more on the menu than tacos, so they were on a real honest-to-God date. That didn't mean he was going to stop giving her grief, though. "Come on, sugar. I'll make you feel good—again."

"You're out of control." She bit her lip. "I like it."

He *felt* out of control, like one wrong step would send him hurtling into something that was completely out of his realm of experience. The jealousy from earlier hadn't abated. If anything, it was getting worse with each passing heartbeat, because he *knew* this couldn't last forever. The longer it went on, the more the loss bloomed in the back of his mind. He was going to lose her, and he was only just realizing how much he *wanted* her.

He didn't want this to end.

Adam stared across the table at her, the realization a weight in his chest threatening to drown him. He couldn't tell if it was a good thing or a bad thing. All he knew was that his life would be a sad specter without Jules in it. He opened his mouth to tell her that, but a shadow fell over their table.

"If it isn't the cute couple."

For fuck's sake. Adam sat back and crossed his arms over his chest. "Grant. You know, you and Jules aren't together anymore — haven't been for years. Why the hell do you keep showing up every time I turn around? Stalking is frowned upon in these parts — not to mention illegal."

Grant narrowed his eyes. "Jules and I are friends, aren't we, Jules?"

"Actually — "

"I just came over to say congratulations. You've convinced me."

"Great." Adam rolled his eyes. "Of what?"

Grant looked from him to Jules and back again. "That you're dating. A friend of mine saw you in, shall we say, a compromising position not more than an hour ago on the side of the road like a common — "

Adam felt like the top of his head was going to explode. "Boy, I suggest you don't finish whatever you were about to say. I'm taking my lady out to a nice dinner, and you're over here, fucking that shit up. Leave."

"Yeah, well, I was just going." Grant turned to leave, muttering, "I could never get her to fuck me in *my* truck."

Adam didn't make a decision to move. One second he was staring at the little pissant's back, and the next he was on his feet and grabbing Grant's collar. "Let's take a walk."

"Adam!"

He ignored Jules, walking Grant out of the restaurant by his throat and giving him a shake for good measure. "In what world would you think I'm the kind of man to let you talk about my woman like that?" Another shake. "Here's a hint—I'm not."

Jules burst through the door. "Adam, stop! Adam, he's turning purple."

He tightened his grip on Grant's neck. "This is the last time I'm going to say this, so I suggest you keep from passing out long enough to hear it. Stay the fuck away from Jules. If you haven't noticed, she doesn't like you. She's too good of a person to say that, but I'm not. You do or say something to hurt her feelings again, and I'll put you in the fucking hospital."

He let go. Grant dropped to his knees, clutching his throat. "What the hell is wrong with you?"

He already knew, before he turned to her, that she wasn't talking to Grant. Adam growled. "We're leaving." He didn't give her a chance to argue, hooking an arm around her waist and practically carrying her away from her wheezing ex.

They were in the truck when she spoke next. "We just walked out on our bill."

"I'll go by tomorrow and take care of it." There was no way he trusted himself to be within punching distance of Grant. Adam pulled out of the parking lot so fast, the momentum threw Jules against him. He knew he needed to slow down, to *calm* down, but he couldn't get himself under control.

It felt like the entire night had been one giant avalanche to this point. He'd known it was coming, but he hadn't been able to escape it. Jules was too damn good for him, and if she didn't know it after that clusterfuck, then he was luckier than he deserved.

"Do you trust me?"

She huffed out a breath. "What kind of question is that? Of course I do, even when you're acting like an idiot."

"Good." He turned off the highway, taking a little dirt road that hadn't gotten much use in high school and didn't appear to get much now. The truck bumped and shook over the potholes, but eventually spit them out in a field with nothing around for miles. "Come on." He got out, grabbed the two blankets from beneath his seat, and walked around to lower the tailgate. Jules followed, but she didn't look too happy with him. He laid the blankets out in the bed of his truck and turned to her. "I'm sorry. I was out of line."

"You think?" She frowned up at him. "What *was* that? I know Grant's an awful person, but he's not worth getting brought up on assault charges."

He let go of the steering wheel and realized his hands were shaking. "He shouldn't have said that about you."

"You're right. He shouldn't. But they're just words."

Except he'd seen her face the moment she registered what Grant had said. If there'd just been anger present, maybe Adam could have let it go—*maybe*—but there had been shame there, too. He reached for her, slowly, giving her time to decide if she'd let him touch her.

Jules didn't move, allowing him to cup her face. He stroked her cheekbones with his thumbs. "I don't want you to regret what we've done. There's no shame in any of it."

"Guess I can't be scandalous without seeing some negative effects, huh?"

He shook his head. "Take everyone else out of the equation. Do *you* regret what we've done?"

"I…" She sighed. "No. I've managed to become a town scandal, at least temporarily. It's going to change the way people look at me, and that's something. These last couple of weeks with you…I'll always look back on them fondly." Her smile was a little bittersweet. "Though I think I'll keep most of this out of the stories I'll tell my grandbabies one day. They're not exactly appropriate for tiny ears."

There it was again—the ever-present reminder that this thing between them wouldn't last forever. The knowledge that there would be another man Jules would fall in love with, a man who'd put a ring on her finger and who'd be there in the delivery room with her when she delivered their children. A man who'd get to spend the rest of his life by her side.

And it wouldn't be Adam.

His chest clenched so tightly, he couldn't draw a full breath. So he did the only thing he could think of.

He kissed her.

Chapter Twenty-One

There were so many things left to say, but Jules let Adam sweep them both away. She couldn't ignore what he'd done to Grant, just like she couldn't ignore the fact that when he touched her, her entire body lit up. And then he looked at her with those dark eyes and actually *cared* about the things she found important.

God, he cared more than he'd ever let anyone see.

Let me in. Please, just let me past those walls you've built so thickly around yourself.

She couldn't let the words out. They were the keeping kind of things, and he'd told her time and time again that he wasn't staying. Expecting him to suddenly fall for her and change his mind wasn't fair to both of them. *She* was the one messing with the rules after she'd assured him she'd be fine with the boundaries he set.

This was never meant to be more than a crazy footnote in my life.

Except it didn't *feel* like a footnote.

It felt world ending.

So she let him kiss her and she wrapped her arms around his neck, needing to be as close as they could be to settle the fears rising in the back of her mind.

Fears that, when he walked away, he'd take a bloody piece of her heart with him.

He lifted her onto the tailgate. "Let me make love to you, sugar. Just this once."

Her heart leaped into her throat, blocking the words she had no business so much as thinking. Jules nodded, because there was nothing else left to say that wouldn't ruin it. She felt absurdly like crying as he pulled off her boots and lifted her dress over her head. "Adam—"

"There's time for that tomorrow."

He was right. They had tonight, and everything could wait for sunrise. She nodded. "Okay."

"Good." He stripped quickly and set both their clothes in the bed of the truck. Then he kissed her again, backing her up and laying her flat on the blankets. "Never lose *you*, sugar." His lips brushed the sensitive spot behind her ear. "There isn't anyone like you out there—I've been around the block enough times to know—and the world would be a dimmer place if you compromised any part of yourself to appease someone else." He eased her bra off, his lips moving over her skin, saying words she never knew she wanted to hear. "You're better than a goddamn eight-second ride, Jules Rodriguez, and I'll never meet your like again."

She started to say…God, she didn't even know what… but he moved down her body, slipping off her panties and spreading her thighs. "And tonight, you're mine." And then his mouth was there against the most intimate part of her, touching her just as his words had a moment before.

Jules gave herself over to him, letting go of her worries for tomorrow and her irritation over how Adam handled things back at the restaurant. He was like a wild thing, barely tamed. Just like the bulls he loved to ride or the stallions on the ranch. He'd let her cuddle up to him, but one wrong move and someone was going to lose an arm.

Not her. She'd spent enough time with him to be sure of that—he'd never hurt her. But that didn't mean a single thing when it came to the people around her.

"You're thinking too hard."

"I can't help it." Her life would be so much easier if she knew how to turn off her stampeding thoughts.

Adam sighed, his breath on her sensitive skin making her squirm. "Let me help." Then he pushed two fingers into her and sucked her clit into his mouth, setting his teeth against her. The sensation was so intense, it was just this side of pain. Jules's mind went blank, and her body went tight.

"Holy good gracious."

He pumped his fingers slowly, dragging them over that spot inside her. She pressed her heels against the bed of the truck, trying to take him deeper, but he laughed softly and used his free hand to pin her hips. "Not yet, sugar."

"Adam, *please*."

He gave her one long lick. "Are you still thinking too hard?"

"I… What?" She squirmed, but he had full control—just like always. She'd always considered herself an independent woman, but there was something about being at Adam's mercy that flat-out did it for her. She tried lifting her hips again. "More."

"All right, sugar. I'll give you more."

She cried out when he removed his hand, but the unmistakable crinkle of a condom wrapper had her shutting right up. This was good. This was even better. He crawled up her body and settled between her thighs. She wrapped her legs around his waist, arching against him. "Kiss me."

"Bossy." He cupped the back of her head and took her mouth even as his cock slid home.

Something inside her that had been rattled and uncertain settled in that moment of perfection. *We have the now. Stop asking for more than he's willing to give. He said I'm his for tonight, and that'll have to be enough.*

But she needed more. Jules dragged her nails down his back. "You make me so hot and crazy and *gah*."

"Tell me more." He began to move, the slightest strokes that drove her to distraction but nowhere near enough to send her over the edge.

"I was *okay*." She dug her fingers into his ass, pulling him deeper. "Mostly okay. Somewhat okay."

"Mmm." He nibbled on her neck, keeping up that infuriating movement.

She couldn't catch her breath. "One look, Adam. That's all it takes. You give me that look and I'm ready to drag you into the nearest enclosed space and drop my panties."

"Good." He picked up his strokes, withdrawing almost all the way out before pushing back into her. "Because I feel the same fucking way, sugar. Every time I stop moving for more than five seconds, all I can think about is the feel of you beneath me, taste you on my tongue, and smell your coconut shampoo. It drives me fucking insane."

"I'm sorry," she gasped.

"I'm not. I fucking love it." He hitched her leg higher on his waist, driving deeper yet. "And the thought of you sharing your future with another man makes it feel like I have fifteen-hundred-pound bull trampling all over my chest." He lowered his voice, so soft that she could barely hear him over the sounds of her breathing. "I want that future. I want it so bad, I can barely stand it."

She started to say...something...but he was already moving, flipping her over and drawing her up onto her hands and knees. "But tonight is mine, sugar. And I'm going to make sure you never forget me."

Forget him? *Impossible.*

He slammed into her, driving a cry from her lips. And then there was no more time for talking. She clutched the blankets, shoving back against him even as he gripped her hips tighter, the sound of flesh meeting flesh joining the cricket sounds in the field around them. "Touch yourself, sugar. I want to feel you come around my cock."

She obeyed without thought, sliding her hand between her legs and stroking her clit. Combined with him filling her, it didn't take long for the first spasms to start. "*Adam.*"

"That's right. Take it all." He slammed into her again and again, driving her out of her mind with pleasure, until she was sure she couldn't take it anymore. Only then did his strokes become irregular, and he let himself go with a curse.

He collapsed next to her, pulling her back against his chest. She stared up at the sky, a blanket of stars that somehow made this even more intimate.

Too soon, her mind kicked back into gear, replaying every single word he'd said since they left the restaurant. She fought to keep her body relaxed, but his sigh proved just how sucky she was at it. "Relax, sugar. We'll talk in the morning."

Maybe. Or maybe that would give him time to reconsider whatever he'd meant when he said he wanted a future with her. She bit her lip so hard it was a wonder she didn't draw blood, barely able to wrap her mind around it.

A future with Adam Meyer.

It was the one thing she hadn't allowed herself to consider. And why would she? He wasn't staying in Devil's Falls.

But what if he did?

Jules liked him—a lot. She liked that he didn't seem to think she was boring or "good ole Jules" or feel the need to patronize her and tell her how he knew better. In fact, he'd done nothing but empower her.

She liked the way he obviously loved his mom. He might

not have spent much time back home over the last decade, but he still cared a whole lot. And Amelia loved her son more than anything else in the world. Jules knew that because she was a shameless eavesdropper when it came to her customers. Amelia was always telling Lenora about Adam's latest escapades with the same tone of voice Jules's mom used to brag about her good grades. It was really sweet.

And there was the sex. Good lord, the sex. It really wasn't fair how out-of-this-world good it was.

He was kind of prickly, but he had a dry sense of humor that she adored. And Aubry didn't scare him. That alone was a big point in his favor. Not to mention, since her best friend hadn't hacked into his cell phone or something else insane, she'd pretty much given her seal of approval. That mattered.

Adam brushed her hair to the side and kissed the back of her neck. "You're doing it again."

"I'm sure I have no idea what you're talking about."

"I'm just as sure that you do." He grabbed the blanket on the other side of her and covered them both with it, settling down again at her back. "It'll all still be there in the morning, sugar. Obsessing about it now isn't going to change a damn thing, except you'll lose sleep."

Easier said than done. She turned in his arms to face him. "Can you do that? Just turn it off?"

His face was little more than a shadow in the darkness. "Some days I'm better at it than others." There was a world of… something…in his voice. Something she didn't have a name for.

She couldn't ask if he was staying. It wasn't the right time, and if he said no, it would just hurt her. So she went with an equally dangerous topic—but one that had nothing to do with her. "You never mention your dad."

"Not much to mention." He sighed. "He was a leaver, as my mama likes to say. He managed to stick around for four years after I was born, but it killed a part of him to be stuck inside these town limits. He rolled back through a couple times as I was growing up, but Mama was never all that happy to see him, knowing she'd see the back of him again before too long. I'm just like him."

He didn't say any of it with anger, more with a quiet fatality she didn't know what to do with. "Adam, there's no such thing as fate. You make your own future."

"You don't understand. I have this…I don't even know what to call it—restlessness, for lack of a better word. It starts in my chest and builds and builds until I feel like I'm coming out of my skin. It's been there ever since I was a kid, and the second I was old enough to get out, it eased the feeling. The only thing that takes it away completely is being on the back of a bull."

How could she compete with that? She'd heard stories about rodeo widows, women who loved a man who loved the rodeo. How could a flesh-and-blood person stand against the roar of the crowd and the adrenaline rush of trying to stay on a rage-filled animal's back for eight seconds? It didn't sound all that wonderful to Jules, but she was unforgivably biased.

Adam leaned against the tailgate. "And now with my mom sick… I just don't know how it's going to end up."

Meaning the cancer could take her.

If it did, not only would Devil's Falls lose one of its favorite ladies, but Adam would lose the last anchor drawing him back to this place. She didn't fool herself for a second into thinking Quinn and Daniel were enough to bring him home, not when he'd be faced with memory after memory of his mother.

And, no matter how she was starting to feel about Adam, *she* would never be enough for him. That was startlingly clear.

"It's okay, Adam. It will be okay."

But the sinking feeling in her chest wouldn't go away. The only thing that had kept him in place for more than two weeks was his mom. If she lost her battle with cancer, he would run as far and fast as he could and not look back.

Chapter Twenty-Two

Adam woke up with a naked Jules in his arms, and hell if that wasn't a way to start the day. He blinked at the bright sunlight and shielded his eyes. She lifted her head. "What time is it?"

"I don't know." He eyed the sky. "Still early. Maybe seven."

"Crap, I have to get going." She sat up, giving him the view of a lifetime, and grabbed her dress. "I open the café today."

As much as he wanted to pull her back down and lose himself in her for a few hours, she was right. Responsibilities waited. His mama had a doctor's appointment today, and he was determined to bully her into letting him go with her. He sat up and stretched. "Let's get you back to town, then."

Jules pulled on her dress and sent him a grin he felt right through his chest. "Last night was something else."

"Yeah, it was."

Her smile dimmed. "But we *do* have to talk about Grant at some point. He was a jackass last night, but you can't just go around manhandling him because he said something…ill-advised."

Ill-advised about summed it up. "Sure I can." When she frowned, he relented. "Sugar, I'll mind my p's and q's, but I'm not civilized enough to sit back and let him insult you. If that's what you're looking for, I'm not your man."

She yanked on her boots. "Just try not to get arrested, okay? Sheriff Taylor is getting close to retiring, and having to haul you in will do a number on his blood pressure."

He finished buttoning his jeans and pulled her into his arms. "You know, Quinn said the same damn thing to me back at the bonfire. Clearly I have a reputation if you all are so worried I'm going to give the good old sheriff a heart attack."

"Well, if he caught sight of what kind of trouble we've been getting into in your truck, I think that's a very real risk."

Adam laughed. "You spend an awful lot of your time taking care of other people."

"Some people don't have anyone to take care of them." She ducked out of his hold when he went for a kiss. "Morning breath!"

"I think we've already established I have a solution for that."

"Good point." She bounded around the side of his truck, reappearing a few seconds later with the fresh bottle of water he'd put in there yesterday, toothbrush, and toothpaste. "You know, I'm not really a fan of camping out, but this has been fun." She shot a look at the bed of his truck, covered with rumpled blankets. "Or maybe I've been listening to too many country songs."

"No such thing." He waited for her to brush her teeth and then followed suit. "Everything worth knowing can be found in a country song."

"I thought the saying was that 'everything I need to know in life, I learned in kindergarten'?"

He grinned. "That, too."

The drive back into Devil's Falls passed in comfortable silence, Jules cuddled up against him. The words he'd said—and hadn't said—last night were a jumbled mess in his chest. He would lose her if he didn't find a way to say what needed to be said—then actually put those words into action—and he didn't want to lose her. He pulled up behind her shop and put the truck into park. "Sugar, I have something to say."

She went still against him. "I'm listening."

"I don't know what the future will hold—"

"No one does."

He waited, and she ducked her head.

"Whoops. You're saying your thing and I'm interrupting."

"I know it hasn't been that long, but I can't imagine my life without you." He opened his mouth to tell her that he wouldn't leave, that he'd do his damnedest to be the man she wanted, but he couldn't force the words out. Despite everything, they still felt like a lie. Instead, he said, "I don't know what's going to happen, and I can only take things one day at a time, but I want you, sugar. Just you."

When she looked up at him, her eyes were shining with unshed tears, her expression looking almost...worried. "Oh, Adam." She kissed him, a quick brushing of her lips against his, and then she was gone, slipping out of his truck and practically running inside.

He stared at the door for a long time. "That went...well." She hadn't told him to fuck off, but she hadn't exactly seemed happy, either. He glanced at the clock. Dealing with Jules's weird reaction would have to wait—he had to leave now if he wanted to be on time for his mom's appointment. Thank God Devil's Falls was so small or he *would* be late.

The doctor's office was a tiny little building off Main Street, and Dr. Jenkins had been practicing long enough that he'd treated Adam's mom when she was a kid. The man was ninety if he was a day, but Mama wouldn't hear of going to someone else. There *was* no one else in town, and she didn't like the thought of going into Odessa more than strictly necessary.

He walked through the door and froze, feeling like he'd just come through a portal into the past. The same faded posters hung on the walls—all cute baby animals with affirming statements—and the same faded blue fabric covered the uncomfortable seats. The receptionist had changed, though. It used to be John's mom that worked here, but the whole family had moved away after his death.

Not that Adam blamed them. Sometimes it was easier to leave the past behind than to face it, day in and day out, while the walls slowly closed in and suffocated any chance of happiness a person had.

The woman behind the desk smiled brightly. "What can I do to help you?"

"I'm looking for Amelia Meyer."

"I'm sorry, sir, I can't give out that information." But the slight shift in her posture told him all he needed to know. His mom had beat him here. Hell, she'd probably moved up the appointment, hoping that he'd miss it altogether.

He eyed the door leading back to the appointment rooms. If he remembered correctly, there were two total. He was so goddamn tired of getting information secondhand from his mama, especially since she tended to sugarcoat everything to the point where it was damn near a lie. He wasn't sure if she was trying to protect him or herself, but he needed to hear what was going on straight from the medical source.

"Excuse me." He turned and strode through the door.

"You can't go back there!"

Too late. He was already past the first open exam room and walking into the second one. His mom and Dr. Jenkins jumped, the former looking as guilty as a sinner in church. Adam shut the door on the squawking receptionist. "Mama."

"Son." She crossed her arms over her chest and lifted her chin. "You're early."

"And yet somehow I was almost late." He ambled over and sat in the spare chair, pinning the doctor with a look. "Bring me up-to-date."

Dr. Jenkins was a nice man who specialized in pediatrics. He hadn't known what to do with Adam as a kid, and he didn't know what to do with him now. He adjusted his glasses, what was left of his white hair standing out against his dark skin. "Now, Adam, you know I can't do that without Amelia's permission."

Her sigh was defeated enough to give Adam a twinge. His mom stood and straightened her dress. "You go ahead and tell him what he needs to know, Matthew. Though you'll have to excuse me. I don't need to hear this again." She walked out of the room with the dignity of a queen, which only made Adam feel even more like an asshole.

He turned to Dr. Jenkins. "I'm sorry for barging in, but she won't give me a straight answer."

"Yes, I'm well acquainted with Amelia's stubbornness." He gave Adam a look over the top of his glasses. "It's a family trait, if I remember correctly." Dr. Jenkins sat back and rubbed a hand over his face. "I won't mince words with you, Adam. It's bad. It took her a long time to admit that what she was feeling wasn't just age, and by that time the cancer had been at work for God alone knows how long."

Adam had to force the words out. "How bad?"

"She's got stage-four lung cancer." Dr. Jenkins's entire being came across as sympathetic. "She's refused chemotherapy, and I don't know that I'd recommend it considering her age and overall health. Unfortunately, the cure for cancer is sometimes worse than the cancer itself, and I believe that would be the case with your mother."

He heard the words, but he couldn't process them. He'd

known it was bad. Of course he'd known it was bad. But bad and fatal were two different things. He swallowed, the motion doing nothing to help his dry throat. "If she'd come in earlier, would it have made a difference?"

"There's no way to tell."

Which wasn't a no. His chest was so tight, he couldn't draw a breath. *My fault. If I'd been home, I would have known something was wrong. I would have made her come to the doctor. It would have made a difference.*

"It's not your fault."

Dr. Jenkins had always seen too much of Adam. As a teenager, he hadn't wanted the man's sympathy. As an adult, he didn't deserve it. He pushed to his feet, weaving a little. "Thanks for telling me."

"Adam—"

"I'll see you around, Doc." He sidestepped the older man and walked out of the room. His mama wasn't there waiting, but he didn't expect her to be. She was pissed he'd barged in, probably pissed that he'd shone the hard light of day onto her situation and forced her to face it. His mama had always been great at self-denial. She denied that his dad leaving had hurt her, just went on without a hitch in her step. But when he was seventeen he'd caught her holding a faded photograph and crying like her heart was breaking. This wasn't any different.

Except heartbreak wouldn't kill her.

Cancer would.

He hit the door to the outside and started walking, bypassing his truck. He wasn't in a good place to be getting behind the wheel right now, and walking might help him get his head on straight—doubtful, but anything was better than standing still right now. He didn't have a destination in mind, but he wasn't particularly surprised to find himself standing in the doorway to Cups and Kittens. Jules was busy with a few other customers, so he took a seat in the corner—the same one Aubry always seemed to be camped out in. Almost immediately, one cat jumped up onto the table in front of him, and a second made itself at home in his lap. Adam stared down at the long-haired orange cat and gave it a tentative pet. When he was rewarded with a purr loud enough to be a jet engine, he did it again. The monstrous feeling inside him didn't uncoil, but he managed to draw his first full breath since hearing the news.

His thoughts tumbled over themselves as he tried to come up with a solution—any solution—to this impossible situation. This wasn't something he could just power his way through until the world rearranged itself to suit him. This was his mother's health. Even if she was willing to do the treatment, Dr. Jenkins hadn't seemed optimistic that it would be worth the cost.

Which meant there was little they could do.

"Adam?"

He didn't look up. If he did, she'd see the pain he couldn't manage to mask on his face, and then she'd ask him if he was okay, and he'd lose it. "I've got to go."

He carefully set the orange cat on the table and walked away.

Chapter Twenty-Three

Jules waited all of a heartbeat before she followed Adam out onto the street. He wasn't exactly a sharer, but she'd have to be blind not to see the pain written over every line of his body. "Adam, wait!"

He stopped, but he didn't turn to face her. "Now's not a good time, sugar."

Her realization last night settled in her chest, feeling like it'd cemented her heart into place. There was no reason to be surprised he was shutting her out. Hadn't he done it every single time she'd asked him what was wrong? But she took a deep breath, shored up her courage, and said, "You can talk to me."

He still didn't turn around. "Talking never did anybody a damn bit of good."

"You won't know until you try." She touched his arm, trying to quell the panic rising with each breath. *Please don't shut me out. Please just talk to me. Please show me that we weren't doomed before we started.*

Adam jerked his arm out of her grasp. "Talking is all

anyone in this shitty little town likes to do—except when it counts. Then everyone shuts the fuck up. So, no, sugar, I'm not going to pour my heart out to you to make you feel better about yourself."

She stumbled back a step, her heart dropping to her stomach. "That's not why I offered to talk."

"Isn't it? You want to fix me, and you want reassurance that I fit into the plans you have for your future. Well, I can't give you either." He started to turn away. "And I'm never going to be the man who will settle down with you."

The woman she was a month ago would have let him walk away. She would have mourned the end of things, but she wouldn't have had the fire burning in the pit of her stomach driving her to chase him down the sidewalk. "No one can fix you, Adam Meyer. Not until you're ready to hold still long enough to realize that your inability to stay in one place has nothing to do with your dad and everything to do with *you*. You're a self-fulfilling prophecy, and you could change if you wanted to."

He glared, his hands clenched at his sides. "Really, Jules? Changing my entire life around to suit your needs isn't as easy as coming up with some quirky plan to scandalize a small town before you move on with your life."

"That's not fair."

But he wasn't listening. "Here's a piece of advice—being the town scandal comes with more strings attached than you want to deal with. It's better to leave the whole damn thing behind."

"There you go again, running the second it looks like you're in danger of putting down roots. Brave, Adam. Really brave."

He shook his head. "This was a mistake. I should have seen it earlier."

This is it. He's not even waiting to leave town to walk away from me. She stared at his back as he moved away from her. "Fine. Walk away from me. It's what you're good at." His step hitched, and for one endless moment, she thought he might turn around, might come back and actually *talk* to her.

But then the moment passed and Adam kept walking.

Jules's breath whooshed out, and it took everything she had not to crumple into a ball on the street and start crying. When the heck had she started to care about that man so much? She was an idiot, and quite possibly insane. She turned, feeling like she was walking through molasses, and looked straight into Grant's gray eyes. *And I thought today couldn't get any worse.*

He smiled. "Trouble in paradise?"

Did he think she cared about what he thought when her heart was walking away from her, the pain cutting deeper with each step he took? She'd thought herself in love with Grant back in the day, but it hadn't been a drop in the ocean compared to what she felt for Adam. So Jules lifted her chin and stared down her nose at her ex. "Here's a tip, Grant—fuck off." She marched into her café and shut the door behind her.

It was clear from the expressions on the handful of customers around that they'd seen and/or heard everything. She tried for a smile. "Does anyone need a coffee refill?"

Mrs. Peterson walked over and took her hands. "I'm so sorry, honey. But after Grant, you really should have known better."

The walls around her seemed to be moving closer. She carefully extracted her hand. "Adam is nothing like that… that…*douchecanoe.* How dare you even compare them? He's stubborn to the point of idiocy and proud and in pain, but that's no reason to put him in the same box." In a distant part of her mind, she knew she was ranting, but she couldn't seem to stop. "And for God's sake, I'm twenty-six. Just because I've been dumped unceremoniously twice in my life doesn't mean

I'm doomed to be alone, and I'll thank you—and everyone else in this town—kindly to remember that. At the very least I should have three shots to get it right before you regulate me to the shelf!"

She strode across the room and through the door into the back, not looking at anyone for fear of seeing more pitying looks. Jamie jumped about ten feet when she barged in, but Jules ignored her cousin and just kept walking, up the stairs and into her apartment. Aubry jumped nearly a foot in the air when she walked through the door, but her surly expression disappeared the instant she saw Jules. "What happened?"

It took two tries to get the words out. "Adam and I are over."

Aubry straightened, her amber eyes narrowing. "You were fine three hours ago. What did he do? Do I have to get out my body-burying kit?"

She was only half sure Aubry was joking. It didn't make her feel any better that her friend was willing to go to such lengths for her. "If you go to jail, I won't have anyone."

"That's not true. Your parents love you very much, even if they live a million miles away, and your extended family is as meddling as they are numerous." She huffed. "Though I guess they're pretty cool, too."

"Aubry…" She stumbled over and sank onto the couch. "Something happened—something bad. I knew he was leaving—I couldn't escape that fact—but I thought we had more time. Maybe I'm asking too much. I just want him to let me in, but it feels like he shuts me out of anything that isn't the good parts of him. What kind of relationship is that?"

"I'm not going to pretend I know a damn thing about relationships, but even I know that wanting the whole of someone isn't a bad thing." She glared out the window as if he was standing right there. "He's an idiot. A big-headed, knuckle-dragging, troublemaking idiot. He doesn't deserve you."

That was the problem. She wasn't sure it was the truth. She took a deep breath. "I should have known better. It shouldn't matter so much what the town thinks of me. Instead of coming up with some crazy plan with my fake boyfriend, I should have done what every normal single woman in her twenties does and joined an internet dating site. There's a world outside Devil's Falls, and I'm sure I could find someone who isn't a troll or a serial killer to love me."

"Jules—"

She stood. "I don't want to hear it."

"Too goddamn bad." Aubry grabbed her elbow and yanked her back down onto the couch. "Life is about risk—don't you look at me like that, I know I don't follow that rule—and you took one. And for the last fucking time, you're not boring. A boring woman would have married Grant and been his little wife with no identity of her own. You don't have to be a wild child or fuel for the gossip mill to be unique and amazing, and I'm stopping now before we both start to cry."

She shook her head. "But everybody—"

"I know for a fact that the only person who thinks less of you for the choices you've made is Grant. That's why you get your back up when anyone else says anything remotely close to you being a cat lady or on the shelf or whatever other hot-button terms you don't like."

Aubry had a point. She *knew* Aubry had a point, but it was so hard to agree with her with Adam's words ringing in her ears. Stability. That's what she'd always sought for herself. She'd known Adam wasn't the most stable guy around, but… "He just walked away. He wouldn't even talk to me."

If there was one thing she learned from her parents' twenty-five-year marriage, it was that people had to be able to fight in a relationship and still have the security to know it wasn't the end of things. She didn't have that with Adam. She wasn't sure she ever would, even if their fight hadn't happened today.

"Adam's a broken individual. Trust me, it takes one to know one." Aubry hugged her. "And, just like me, you can't fix him through sheer force of will. The world would be a better place if your sunshine could drown out other people's rainstorms—it just doesn't work like that."

But she didn't want to change him. Not really. She liked all of Adam's hidden depths and a thousand other little things about him. The only thing she wanted was for him to let her in, to let her help him shoulder the burden. If his mom really was terminal, then he'd need someone to lean on. He couldn't do it alone, not without breaking, not when he obviously loved Amelia so much.

But he wouldn't take help from her. She suspected he wouldn't take help from *anyone*.

Or maybe he would…

Jules straightened. "I have to make a call." She disentangled herself from Aubry and pulled her phone out of her pocket. It took all of a second to find Daniel's number and call it.

He answered almost immediately. "Yep?"

"Adam needs you." Her voice broke, but she charged on. "He won't talk to me, but something happened, and he needs to talk to someone."

"Does he know you're calling?"

"No."

Daniel was quiet for a long ten seconds. "We don't talk about some things, Jules. It's just the way it is."

What was it with the men in her life who couldn't deal with emotion? She took a deep breath and tried to keep the strain from her voice. "I know you have unresolved issues— all of you do—but if you let him shoulder this alone, it's going to kill something inside him. Please, Daniel. Please at least try to talk to him."

Her cousin sighed. "I'll try. That's all I can do."

It would have to be good enough. "Thank you." She hung up and turned to find Aubry staring at her. "What?"

"You really fell hard for this guy, didn't you?"

Too hard, too fast, too much all around. She slumped back into the couch. "I really did."

"I think this calls for a tea party." Aubry stood. "And by tea party, I mean we're going to drink vodka out of teacups and eat our weight in ice cream while we bitch about the men who've done us wrong."

"I don't deserve you."

"Aw, Jules, that's where you're wrong. You're better than all of us—you're just too good of a person to see it." She disappeared into her room and came back with two fine china teacups on saucers. "Now, do you want to shoot some noobs, or is this the kind of hurting that requires a sappy romance movie?"

Jules's eyes burned. "You're the best friend anyone could ever ask for."

"Just don't go around telling people that."

"Your secret is safe with me."

Chapter Twenty-Four

Adam didn't have a place in mind when he started driving after grabbing a six-pack from the market, but he ended up in the cemetery, winding through the narrow paths until he stood in front of his friend's headstone. He opened a beer and finally made himself read it.

John Moore
Beloved son and brother
December 16, 1981 — December 16, 2002
It's been too long.

And somehow not nearly long enough.

He opened a second beer and, after a self-conscious look around, upended it on the grass covering his friend's grave.

Adam sighed. His mama wasn't talking to him, and Lenora had practically ripped out his throat when he tried to push the subject. As much as he hated to admit it, she was right—they both needed time to cool off. The problem was the truth wasn't going anywhere, no matter how many laps he drove around town.

She's really going to be gone for good, long before I'm ready to let her go. I don't know that I'll ever be ready to let her go.

His mama was the closest thing to roots he had in this life. What was he going to do without that? It didn't matter that he didn't see her all that often normally—knowing she was carrying on life in Devil's Falls had always steadied him, just a bit.

"So what's brought you out here looking for answers?"

He took a long pull of his beer and turned to where Daniel approached. He wasn't ready to talk about it. He didn't know if he'd ever be ready to say it aloud. So he went with something easier to bear. "You know, John was one of my best friends, and I've never come out here to visit him."

"He's gone. Visiting his grave doesn't make him any less gone."

The words didn't sit well with him. There was nothing more final than a gravestone, and the thought that in too short a time he might be standing in front of a different gravestone made his throat burn. "Have you been out here?"

"Yeah." Daniel tipped back his head and closed his eyes. "I share a six-pack with him once a month."

It was becoming startlingly clear that Adam had well and truly fucked up when he left town—and he'd been fucking up ever since. "I should have come back sooner. I should have been here for you and Quinn."

And for Mama.

"We were all fighting our own demons in our own way. You did the best you could."

But that wasn't the truth. He could have done better. Oh, he'd spent the last decade telling himself that no one expected any different from him. He was just like his old man. The bad egg. The hell-raiser. So when he blew out of town, restlessness driving him like a leaf before a hurricane, it was only the last in a long list of things adding up to him being the piece-of-shit leaver he'd always known he was.

He'd never once considered that he could change.

"My mama's dying. Cancer."

Daniel finally looked at him. "Shit, I'm sorry. I didn't know."

"No one did. The only reason *I* know is that I bullied my way into her doctor's appointment." And suddenly the words were there where there hadn't been any before. "I should have been here. All this time, I should have been here."

"You had your reasons for leaving."

Adam suddenly hated that everyone was so goddamn willing to give him a pass. "What could possibly be more important than being here? All these years wasted, chasing some adrenaline high while I was missing the shit that really mattered back home."

"Fuck, Adam, what do you want me to say? Was it shitty that you left right after graduation? Yeah, it was. And, yeah, it would have been nice to have you here instead of passing through town like a fucking tumbleweed. But you made the decision that you made. I wasn't willing to lose another friend over it."

Especially not after they'd lost John.

"I'm sorry." He felt like he'd been saying that too fucking much lately. What did sorry really mean if he didn't do a damn thing to keep this shit from happening again?

"There's nothing to be sorry for. We all did stupid shit when we were eighteen and full of more come than common sense. If you keep beating yourself up about it, you're never going to get past it." He looked at Adam. "But you're not eighteen anymore. So what are you going to do?"

About his mama.

About Jules.

About his goddamn life in general.

He rubbed a hand over his face. That was the problem—like Daniel said, they weren't eighteen anymore. He'd spent so long running from the idea of settling down, he wasn't sure what it'd be like to stand and fight. But he already knew that chasing down his favorite adrenaline rush was only a temporary solution. "I don't know."

"Here's a hint—apologize. Your mama loves you as much as you love her." Daniel pushed to his feet and finished off his beer. "And, Adam, none of us knew she was sick—not like you're saying. If no one in Devil's Falls could tell, how the hell would you be able to? Do you have some sort of X-ray vision that you've neglected to tell me about?"

"No."

"Yeah, I didn't think so." He awkwardly squeezed Adam's shoulder. "Just be there for her. That's all she wants."

That seemed to be all anyone wanted from him. Except Jules. Jules fully expected him to leave at some point and had plans to eventually settle down with some future guy.

Something must have showed on his face, because Daniel hesitated. "I hate to even ask, but what the hell happened with Jules? One second you're making googly eyes at her, and the next she's calling me upset and telling me to track your stupid ass down."

Of course she'd been the one to call Daniel. It didn't matter that he'd said some awful shit to her—she was still trying to take care of him. "It never would have worked. I don't deserve her."

But he wanted to.

Daniel leveled a long look at him. "Yeah, well, not with you being own self-fulfilling prophecy. You're not your old man. You never were, though you've been determined to prove otherwise since you were a kid." He set the empty bottle back into the six-pack. "Let me know if there's anything I can do to help with your mom." And then he was gone, striding across the cemetery to where his truck was parked at the entrance.

The possibility that he wasn't his father 2.0 had never really occurred to Adam. Oh, he'd fantasized about making different choices when he was too young to know better, but when push came to shove, his instincts were always to walk away. To pursue the next adrenaline rush. Adam glared at the horizon, waiting to feel the pull for the next ride, the next highway to nowhere.

For once in his life, it didn't have the same siren call as what was behind him—Devil's Falls, his mama, and Jules.

"Better late than never." He headed for his truck. He wasn't sure where to start, but he owed his mama an apology. He'd mishandled things, and having the best of intentions didn't change the fact that he'd pissed her off something fierce.

The drive back to her place passed in a blur, and then he was striding into the kitchen, where his mama and Lenora were puttering over of pot of what smelled like chicken noodle soup. Lenora took one look at his face and said, "I'll be in the living room if you need me."

He wanted to tell her that his mama didn't need her for a conversation with her son, but it was right that Lenora stood with her against the world—even him. His mama had stood alone for far too long, and he was honestly glad that she'd found happiness in the midst of everything. "Mama."

She braced her frail shoulders like she was going to war and turned to face him. "Son."

He didn't want to fight. Fuck, he was so tired of fighting. "I wish you would have told me."

"That was my choice to make."

"Mama—"

"I don't know if it helps or makes it worse, but I haven't known nearly as long as you seem to think." She shot a look at the doorway Lenora had disappeared through. "She wouldn't take no for an answer when it came to contacting you."

He exhaled. She hadn't hid it from him. Not really. That was just his knee-jerk reaction upon hearing that she had stage-four cancer. It had never occurred to him that it had surprised her as much as him. *Great job being sympathetic, ass.* "I've made a mess of things."

"You're overprotective." She smiled. "There are worse things, especially when I can't blame your bullheadedness on your father."

He managed a smile, though it felt brittle. "I don't know how to do this. I don't know how to be there for you without stepping on toes and trying to *fix* things."

"Oh, baby." She crossed the tiny kitchen and took his hands. "Some things you can't fix, no matter how hard you try. I was never going to make it out of this life alive. None of us are." She hugged him. "Give me the benefit of choosing how I'm going out. I don't want the chemo. The cancer is doing enough to me, and I can't bear the thought of my body wasting away any faster than it already is."

Stubborn to the very end.

Just like me.

It struck him that he'd been so focused on his old man that he'd never really considered what he'd inherited from his mama. If his father was a leaf on the wind, his mama was as steady as the sunrise. *I could have learned a thing or two from her if I'd just held still long enough to realize that.* He didn't know how to prove to her that he was determined to change, but there was only one place to start. "I'm going to buy a house."

His mama's eyes went wide. "What?"

"It's time. If you don't want chemo, I'm not going to push you. It's your decision. But I'm going to be here every step of the way and I'm going to help how I can."

Her grip tightened on his hands. "And after?"

That was the question, wasn't it? Daniel's words echoed

through his mind.

You're not eighteen anymore.

It's time to stop acting like a scared kid.

"I hear the Rodriguez ranch needs help. Daniel would be more than happy to put me to work."

A shake passed through her body. "Truly?"

How had he never seen how much his leaving hurt his mama? *Selfish to the core.* Adam hugged her, holding her as tightly as he dared. "I'm not leaving again." If he could give his mom something, he'd give her this. He pressed a quick kiss to the top of her head. "What I think we both like to forget is that I had two parents. I'm tired of following in the footsteps of that piece of shit."

"Language."

"Sorry, Mama. My point is that maybe I could learn a thing or two from the better half of the equation."

Her smile was a reward all its own. "You're a good man, baby."

It was the first time she'd ever said that to him, and if he didn't quite believe her, not yet, he was determined to make it the truth. He let go of her and stood back, his mind already turning to how he'd make a real life for himself here. He had a ton of money saved up because he'd stopped blowing through it after the first year of bull riding and had lived pretty low-key in the meantime—more than enough for a down payment.

"Baby?"

"Yeah, Mama?"

"What are you going to do about the Rodriguez girl?" Some censure had leaked back into her tone. "I was by Cups and Kittens earlier today, and she looks like she got hit by a truck." There was no doubt in her mind that he was the cause, and he couldn't even get pissed because it was the damn truth.

He'd well and truly fucked up.

"I'm going to make it right." He didn't know how, and

he'd more than deserve it if Jules told him to take a hike while she moved on with her life. Adam didn't give a fuck. He'd fallen for her, and he'd do whatever it took to fix things and prove to her that he was the perfect man for her. He just had to figure out how.

His mama patted him on the arm. "You better. She's a good girl. I think she'd make an excellent daughter-in-law."

He laughed. "Yeah, well, let's take things one day at a time."

"That's the only way you can take them, baby." She kissed him on the cheek. "Now, go get your woman."

Chapter Twenty-Five

Jules spent the week after breaking up with Adam in a strange haze. She did everything she could think of to snap out of it, but nothing worked. Not riding, not playing bloodthirsty video games with Aubry, not cuddling her cats. Nothing. She caught herself thinking about Adam half a dozen times a day, wondering if he was okay or if the pressure had gotten to be too much and he'd left town.

It hurt to think of never seeing him again.

It hurt worse to think of running into him randomly on his visits back in town.

Everything hurt.

She'd tried to comfort herself by promising herself that she'd find someone else, that she'd finally take the leap and sign up for internet dating, but the words were just that—words. They didn't comfort her in the least. She'd sat for an hour and just stared at the registration page before closing the browser completely. What did some guy on the other side of a screen have that made jumping through the required hoops worth it?

Would he give her dirty-talking lessons or, even better, would he hold her close and whisper things that made her hot and twisty without laying a finger on her? Would he get Aubry's stamp of approval and seem to actually enjoy going toe-to-toe with her? Would he make love to Jules in the bed of his truck beneath a summer sky?

And if he managed to achieve that herculean feat... would she be picturing Adam the entire time?

The more she thought about it, the more she had to face the facts—Adam Meyer had well and truly ruined her for anyone else.

She checked the clock, breathing a sigh of relief that she could finally close. There hadn't been anyone in for over an hour, but she didn't like to keep changeable hours. People depended on her being open the hours that were posted, and doing otherwise just didn't sit right with her, whether there were customers or not. She stepped over where Ninja Kitteh was lounging in the middle of the floor and walked to the door to lock it.

And froze.

Adam stood on the other side of the glass, looking even better than she remembered. Her heart leaped into her throat, and she had to clench her hands to keep from opening the door and throwing herself into his arms. *He walked away. Just because he didn't actually leave town in the last week doesn't change a single thing.* She had to remember that, though it was hard to with him looking at her like he'd been in the desert for weeks and she was an oasis.

"Can I come in?"

She didn't have to be able to hear him to know what words his lips formed. Numb, she nodded and opened the door. *Stupid. So freaking stupid.* But she'd proven time and again that she didn't have a lick of common sense when it came to this man. "Hi."

"Hi." He looked down as Khan came and rubbed himself on Adam's legs, purring furiously. "How are things?"

Awful. Terrible. No good. "Great."

"Good." He gave in to the cat's demanding and picked him up. Khan looked at Jules, smug as all get-out. As well he should be—he was in Adam's arms and she was standing just out of reach.

She was in the lowest of low places if she was jealous of a *cat.* "Great."

"You said that." A small smile quirked the edges of his lips, and she wasn't sure if she wanted to kiss him or smack him for walking back in here and making her heart break all over again.

She crossed her arms over her chest. "What do you want, Adam? Because I think you made your position pretty freaking clear the other day."

"Come for a drive with me."

"What?" She'd braced herself for him to say a lot of things, but that hadn't even been on the list. Adam was a lot of things, but cruel wasn't one of them. "Absolutely not."

"Please, sugar. I want to show you something."

"Is it a hole in the ground where you're going to stuff my dead body?"

He shot her a reproachful look. "It's funny—your mouth is moving, but I'm hearing the redhead talking."

Probably because Aubry was a hell of a lot smarter than Jules. She had things down. She stayed inside and interacted with people solely on her own terms—with the safety net of a computer between them. *She* wouldn't be standing here, seriously considering going somewhere with a man who'd broken her heart. "Adam, I can't do this. I'm barely getting through as things stand, and taking a drive with you is only going to make it worse. I don't think I can survive another go-round."

Instantly the smile was gone from his face. "I'm sorry for that, sugar. I really am. Let me make it up to you."

I can't. It would be a mistake of epic proportions. "No."

"You're really putting a wrench in my grand gesture, you know that?" He sighed. "I guess we'll have to do this a different way."

She blinked. "Uh, what?"

"Come here." He pulled out his phone and started typing.

What the heck is going on? She slowly crossed the distance between them, feeling like she was approaching a rabid animal. He'd either run or attack, and she wasn't sure which would be preferable at this point.

"Here." He hooked her waist and pulled her into the circle of his arms, turning her so her back met his chest. She was so distracted by the sheer presence of him and the longing the feeling of him touching her awoke that she almost didn't realize he was trying to show her his phone screen. Jules frowned at it. "That's one of those house-finding apps." She liked to search them when she was bored, though she had no reason to move from the comfy little apartment above the café.

His chuckle made her shiver. "Look at the house."

It was a cute little thing. Two bedrooms, one and a half baths. Just outside town on twenty acres. It needed some love and probably a few months' worth of renovations, but it had promise. Her chest ached, something like hope sprouting there. "Why am I looking at a house?"

"I bought it yesterday." His breath ghosted over her ear. "Or at least I started the process of buying it. That shit takes forever. But the earnest money is in place, and assuming all the paperwork goes through, it'll be mine just inside of thirty days."

The screen started to blur before her eyes. "You're buying a house."

"I'm buying a house." He turned her in his arms, his hands on her hips. "I'm staying, sugar. I've been running for my entire life, and I finally found a reason to stop."

"Your mom."

His eyes were intense on hers. "She plays into it, I'm not going to lie. But you're the one who made me stand still long enough to realize what I'd be missing if I left again. Devil's Falls isn't perfect, but it's got one point in its favor that no other town I've ever been to has."

"What's that?"

"You." His hands flexed on her hips like he wanted to pull her closer. "When I said I'd never met anyone else like you, I was telling the truth. You make this world a better place, and you make me want to be a better man."

They were words she'd wanted to hear so badly, she almost convinced herself that he hadn't actually said them. "But…" She could barely process this 180. She'd been halfway prepared to spend the rest of her life wasting away into spinsterhood, holding close the memories of the last few weeks to keep her warm at night, and now here he was, saying things she never would have dreamed he'd say. So she focused on the—slightly—easier thing. "You bought a house."

"I bought a house." He inched her closer. "And I'm going to be honest with you—someday I want you living there with me. We can take it slow, but if you'll give me a second chance to do this right, that's it for me. You're the one I want, and I fully intend on there being a ring and a couple of babies in the plans."

A ring. Babies. A house. Her heart leaped into her throat, making it hard to get words out. "You don't do anything halfway, do you?"

He grinned. "What's the point?"

Truer words were never spoken. She put her hands on his chest, resisting the last little space between them. "What happened the other day?"

This was it. If he shut her out again, she'd know that his words were just that. She could compromise on a lot of things, but this wasn't one of them.

He rested his forehead against hers. "My mama has stage-four lung cancer. That's why I was losing my shit, and that's what I wouldn't tell you because I could barely stand to think it."

Oh, Adam. "I'm so sorry."

"Me, too."

She took a deep breath, forcing herself to ask the question she really needed answered. "Are you sure you're not just reeling from the news and reacting?"

"Yes, that shit sent me for a loop, but I've found my feet. My mama and I have talked, and I'm working to be as at peace with her decisions as I can be, but that's what they are—her decisions. I'm going to support her and be here for her." He framed her face. "And I'm going to court you good and proper, Jules Rodriguez."

She licked her lips. "Court me?"

"Yep. I've gone and fallen for you, and there's only one right way to go about these things."

She felt like she'd stepped into an alternate dimension—one she wanted so desperately, she could almost taste it. "I'm not dreaming, am I?"

"I sure as fuck hope not."

He was really here. He was really saying these things. He was really willing to fight for her.

Jules hugged him close, putting everything she had into it. "I can't say anything to make the situation with your mom right, but I'll be here for you to lean on when you need it." And she'd do whatever it took to help him cope with the inevitable pain. She didn't want to say the words that rose inside her, but she couldn't leave a single stone unturned when it came to

Adam. "Are you sure this isn't all to make her happy now, and that you'll leave after she's…"

"Gone?" He held her close, propping his chin on the top of her head. Strangely enough, it felt more intimate than anything they'd done up to this point. "I know nothing I say will convince you of this—that I'll have to show you to prove it to you—but I'm not leaving, sugar. If you want to keep your distance until you believe me, that's fine. I'm willing to wait."

It dawned on her that he really would. He'd wait for as long as it took to convince her that this was real and he was earnest. She leaned back. "So, marriage and babies, huh?"

"Eventually." His eyebrows rose. "Though I'm willing to negotiate on the number of rug rats."

"How noble of you."

"Not in the least." He smiled. "I mean to keep you forever, sugar. And when we're old and gray, we can scandalize the folk in Devil's Falls just for the hell of it."

Epilogue

Adam supported his mama's arm as they walked down the aisle to her seat in the front row. She couldn't get around as well these days, but she was determined not to use her chair today. It broke his heart a little bit, but she'd surpassed all the doctor's estimates and was still holding on to her joy of life in the bargain. He couldn't ask for more. "Here we are."

"I'm so proud of you, baby. I don't say that enough."

He helped her into her chair and crouched in front of her so they were almost eye to eye. "It means the world to me every time you do."

Her eyes shone. "I was wrong all those years ago to compare you to that man. I can't help wondering if…"

"No, Mama. I don't have any regrets. If things had been different, maybe I wouldn't be marrying the woman of my dreams today."

She nodded, her mouth trembling up into a smile. "I love you, baby."

"I love you, too. Now sit here and get comfortable — I think we're about to start." He smiled at Lenora as she took her seat next to his mom. "You ladies have your handkerchiefs?"

Lenora laughed and waved him away. "Don't you worry your pretty head about it. I've got us covered."

"Good." He looked at his mama. "You just wait here after the ceremony. I'll be back to walk you to the cars."

"We've got it taken care of." Quinn and Daniel appeared next to him, both dressed to the nines in suits that matched his—black and gray. Daniel pulled him to his feet, and Quinn smiled down at the women. "I'll be your escort to the reception. Be kind—my ego is so delicate."

His mama and Lenora tittered. "You're a good boy, Quinn."

"Nah, I'm just really good at faking it." He turned to Adam. "Get to the altar, man. It's time."

Time. The moment he'd been waiting for since Jules agreed to take him back. He knew she'd been unsure about it at first, but he never wavered. He wanted her. He wanted to be here. Nothing was going to change that—not now, not ever. And things slowly settled down. He got a job working with Daniel on the Rodriguez farm and started renovating his house. Jules moved in after six months, and here they were, a year later, about to make this thing truly official.

He'd never thought he could be so happy.

The music started, the groomsmen and bridesmaids walking down the aisle. There was Quinn walking with Aubry, who looked like she'd rather chew off her own arm than touch him. And Daniel with their other cousin Jamie.

And then the music changed, and there she was. His entire world narrowed down to where Jules stepped out into the aisle, her gaze going directly to him and staying there, her big, beautiful smile striking straight to the heart of him.

Quinn nudged him. "Breathe, man."

Adam inhaled, not realizing he'd been holding his breath. "Thanks."

"No problem."

Jules made her way to him, her dress—a princess dress was what she called it—trailing behind her. She looked like something out of a dream, but she could have been wearing a potato sack for all he cared. She handed her bouquet off to Aubry and took his hands. "Hi."

"Hey."

The pastor started speaking, but it might as well have been Latin. Nothing else mattered but the woman standing before him and the vows they repeated. Vows promising forever, through thick and thin. Vows making it official—he was hers and she was his. He'd heard of idiots getting cold feet at making a promise like that, but Adam had never been more sure of anything in his life.

"You may kiss the bride."

He swept her into his arms and dipped her down into a kiss while their family and friends cheered. He set her back on her feet. "Hello, Mrs. Rodriguez-Meyer."

"Hello, Mr. Meyer." She grinned. "Shall we do this thing?"

"We shall." He offered his elbow to her and they walked back down the aisle, husband and wife. From there it was another blur to the limo until the door shut between them and everyone else.

She stretched her feet out. "Whew, that was crazy. Are you going to think less of me if I kick off my heels and take to the dance floor during the reception? These things are killing my feet."

"I wouldn't dream of it." He pulled her into his lap. "I love you so much, it just blows my mind."

"Good." She kissed him. "Because I love you more."

"Bullshit." He dipped his head and captured her earlobe between his teeth, biting gently. "And you're going to pay for saying so."

"Oh, yeah? How do you plan on doing that?"

His hand was already on the back of her dress, seeking out her zipper. "I have a few ideas."

"Adam! We can't."

"Sugar, I already told the driver to take the long way around."

Her laugh warmed him to the very bottom of his soul. "You dog."

"You better get used to it." He slid her dress down, freeing her breasts. "Because you're not getting rid of me."

"I love you." She gasped when he leaned her back, careful of her perfectly done-up hair. "I love you so much."

"I know, sugar. I love you, too. I'm about to show you just how much."

Acknowledgments

To God: Another year, another book, another set of challenges and rewards I never could have dreamed of. Thank you.

To Heather Howland: It's hard to believe this was the first category series you contracted from me — and the evolution this story has gone through since then. Thank you so much for helping me bring it to life and make it the best story it could be.

To Kari Olson: For always being down for some awesome country music recommendations. My wallet is still weeping, but Adam wouldn't be quite as hot without some serious inspiration behind him. My playlist is killer for this series because of you!

To the Rabble: For being Adam's first cheerleaders and for being so enthusiastic about this series! I hope he rocked your world like he rocked mine!

And to Tim: Yeah, yeah, you knew this was coming. Thank you for being my rock in the storm and for sharing the sleep deprivation so I wasn't a total zombie while working. Love you like whoa!

About the Author

New York Times and *USA Today* bestselling author, Katee Robert, learned to tell stories at her grandpa's knee. Her favorites then were the rather epic adventures of The Three Bears, but at age twelve she discovered romance novels and never looked back. Though she dabbled in writing, life got in the way, as it often does, and she spent a few years traveling, living in both Philadelphia and Germany. In between traveling and raising her two wee ones, she had the crazy idea that she'd like to write a book and try to get published.

Also by Katee Robert...

SEDUCING THE BRIDESMAID

MEETING HIS MATCH

SANCTIFY SERIES

THE HIGH PRIESTESS

QUEEN OF SWORDS

QUEEN OF WANDS

ASK ME NICELY
a novel by Amy Andrews

Veterinarian Sal Kennedy's lost her mojo. On the anniversary of a tragedy, she'll do anything to erase the painful memories, including overdoing the tequila and making a pass at fellow veterinarian Doyle Jackson. He definitely knows how to make her mojo sit up and beg. Now Sal wants more, and she'll play dirty to get it. But Doyle wants more than sex, even if it means fighting just as dirty. Even if it means they both keep losing all their clothes in the process…

Made in the USA
Las Vegas, NV
03 October 2023

78524071R00125